The Book of Secrets and Shadows

THE DREACHEN CODEX
BOOK ONE

WENDY LARKING

WENDY LARKING

THE BOOK OF SECRETS AND SHADOWS

THE DREACHEN CODEX
BOOK ONE

Published by Larking About Press

ISBN: 978-1-916758-02-5 (ebook edition)

ISBN: 978-1-916758-03-2 (Paperback edition)

First edition v1.1, October 2023

Cover by Bailey and Bloom

Editing by Bailey and Bloom

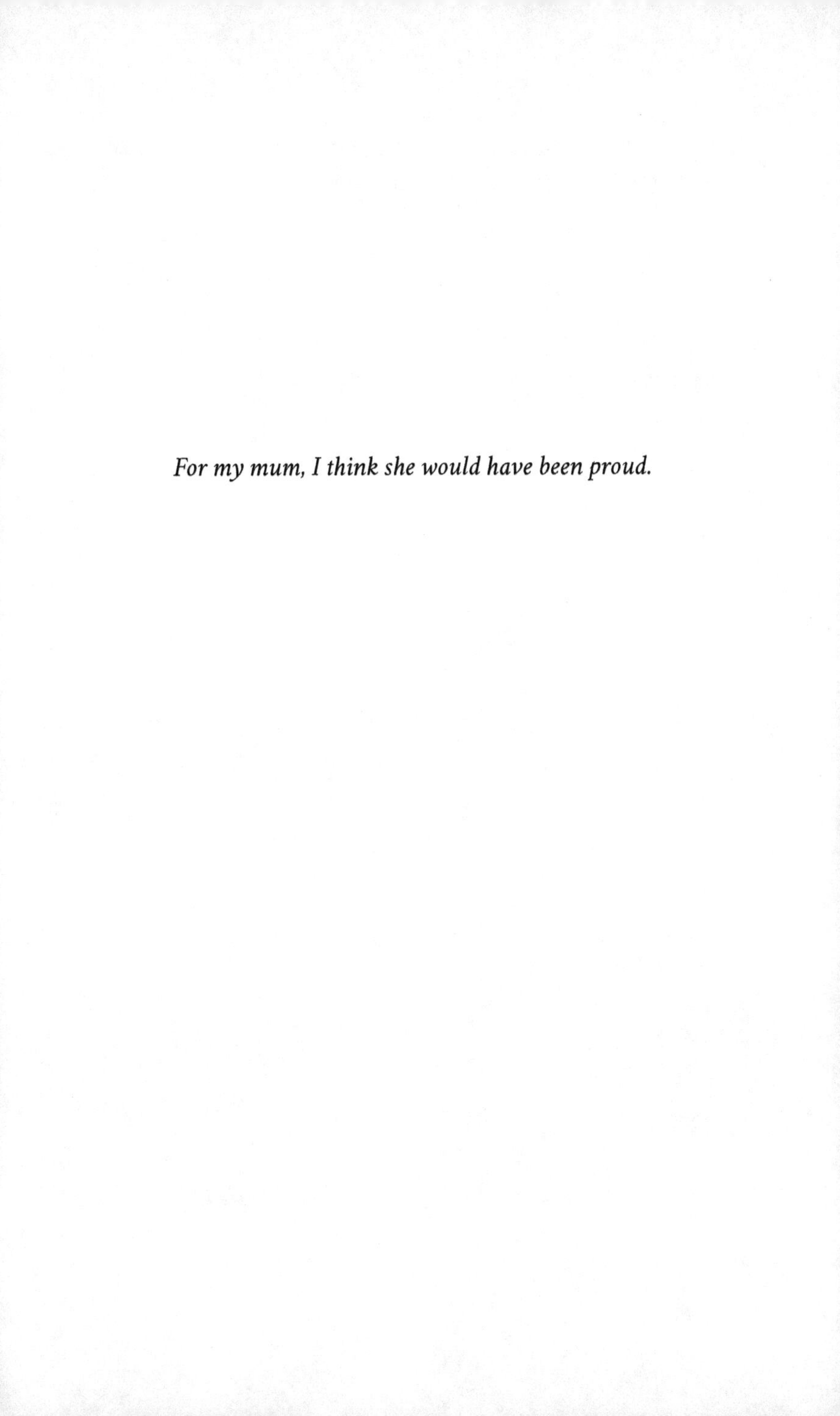

For my mum, I think she would have been proud.

Chapter One

Ember tried to keep herself from squirming as she withstood the scrutiny of the old lady seated in front of her.

"You are very young." The voice was severe, reflecting years of commanding audiences accustomed to such regal surroundings.

"Not quite two and twenty, ma'am," Ember bobbed a curtsey for good measure. "But I have been involved with my father's cases for the last four years." Almost true.

"And your father is not well?"

"No, ma'am, though I am sure he will be better soon." A lie.

Ember knew her father wasn't going to get well, she recognised the signs: the weakness, the coughing, the bouts of delirium. She knew that tuberculosis would take her father sooner rather than later. Just like it had taken her mother when Ember was only ten years old. Since then it had been just herself and her father against the world.

"Has your father trained you himself?"

"Yes, ma'am." Her father was a private investigator, specialising in missing persons, or finding out information. But had never taken her on his special cases. These—always heralded by a black edged card— he investigated alone, just once or twice a year, often disappearing for several days and arriving back exhausted and haggard. These were cases where he took gruesome looking weapons from the black chest he thought she didn't know about. She had discovered the chest under his bed the previous year and it hadn't taken her long to pick the lock, a skill her mother had taught her dressed up as a game. Along with the weapons, the chest held a curious black ring embossed with "VR." Although Ember had tried to question him about the cases, pleaded even, he had not uttered a word. He just repeated that they had to be done and for a while afterwards things always seemed to be a bit easier. Often there was money for a new dress or coat for Ember and they were able to have better cuts of meat for supper.

When the black-edged card stamped with the letters "V" and "R" was delivered earlier that morning, Ember had hid it from her father knowing he would be upset that he wouldn't be able to attend. Her decision to go in his place occurred when she looked at how little coal they had left and how bare the cupboards were. With her father ill, they hadn't taken a new investigation case in months and the bookshop they also ran was not prosperous enough to live on. She had taken the black ring while he had slept, moving rapidly before she could change her mind. It hadn't taken her long to work out that the letters "VR" were for Victoria Regina, the queen's cypher—she had been trained by the best. She hadn't really expected to be admitted to the palace; now she was here she was sure the queen could hear her heart hammering in her chest as she withstood her stern scrutiny.

"Very well. We will give you a trial, until your father is better of course. It's not like we can find anyone else at short notice anyway. Beresford will give you the details." She called out and a gentleman appeared from a door behind her. He looked to be in his forties—her father's age—and he was tanned like he had spent many years in a warm climate, his brown shoulder-length hair showing some grey. He was dressed tastefully in clothes that were good quality but well worn and as he approached, Ember saw he walked with a limp.

His eyes widened when he saw Ember, but he did not speak, standing quietly with his hands behind his back.

"Beresford, give Miss Merrington the details of the case. She will be on trial until Mr Merrington is well enough to resume his services to us."

"Ma'am," he bowed his consent and walked towards Ember. "This way Miss Merrington."

"Thank you, Your Majesty." Ember curtsied again, releasing the breath that had been lodged in her chest , and followed him out.

❖

Beresford shut the door of his office behind Ember and moved over to a desk which stood in the middle of the room. He indicated to the chairs placed in front of the desk.

"Please take a seat."

Ember sat warily, looking round at the opulence—the room was decorated in white with gold cornices; rich red velvet hung in the windows. The ceiling was painted with a biblical scene. The heavy dark wood furniture was so well polished she could only amaze at the amount of work it must take to achieve the high shine. It was a moment before she realised that Beresford was speaking.

"I am sorry to hear about your father, Miss Merrington. I hope he will be better soon."

Ember narrowed her eyes and regarded him. *Did he know her father?* She dare not tell him the truth of his illness. She needed this job badly, so smiling quickly she uttered, "I am sure he will."

Beresford hesitated for a moment, squinting slightly before asking "You don't remember me do you?"

"You have the advantage of me, Mr Beresford. I can't say I do." Ember sifted through her memories but drew a blank; she was sure she had never seen him before. Had he frequented the bookshop?

"Your father and I are old friends, and I also knew your mother." He paused, a sad smile briefly crossing his face. "You are very much like her."

Ember had been told this before with her dark auburn hair and pale freckled complexion. But her hazel eyes were her father's.

"The last time I saw you though, you were about knee high," he said, indicating with his hands and smiling.

"Ah, then there is little wonder I do not remember you, sir. I was just a child then," Ember responded formally; she could not allow him to become familiar. If he knew how ill her father was he would surely tell the queen to find someone else to help. She decided to get straight to the point. "Please tell me about this case, Mr Beresford."

The smile now gone, he nodded. "Very well. Lady Margaret Berthilda Fordingworth has gone missing." She must have looked blankly at him because he continued, "She is a cousin of the queen's late husband."

That would explain the queen's interest in this simple missing person's investigation then. Ember felt more relieved about the case—finding lost people was something she was familiar with.

"And you would like me to find her?" She didn't relish the idea of hunting for frivolous nobility who had probably never had a hard day in their life, but needs must.

"Yes, but the first thing you must do is sign some documents." Beresford shuffled the papers on his desk before pulling out a couple of pages. He didn't hand them over right away, instead keeping two fingers on them to hold them down. His voice took an official tone "Being employed by the queen, in any capacity, requires the utmost secrecy. These documents are to ensure that you do not disclose who you are working for and you do not discuss the case with anyone else. Is that clear?"

"Perfectly, thank you," Ember replied briskly and he pushed them across the desk to her. She glanced over them but there wasn't a chance she wasn't going to sign them—not if she and her father were going to eat.

"When was Lady Fordingworth last seen?" She might as well get on with the case.

"At the Hamiltons' ball, two days ago. She disappeared that night."

"Two days!" Ember exclaimed. " And you've waited until now?"

Beresford had the decency to look a little abashed before replying, "Lady Fordingworth is known for not always behaving in the manner her parents would wish." Ember couldn't prevent herself from rolling her eyes and caught a brief smile from Beresford at her reaction. He continued, "It was only today that her family chose to approach Her Majesty for assistance, after they had checked with all of her friends."

Ember nodded, content that they had at least done that much. She thought for a moment and then asked, "Could I please have a list of all the ball attendees and Lady Fording-worth's friends?"

A look of approval crossed Beresford's face as he nodded. "I will have those drawn up and sent round directly."

Ember was curious, "Have the police been informed? Are they questioning the attendees?"

Beresford fixed her with a weary look, "If we were able to bring the police into this matter then there would be no need for you, Miss Merrington. Her Majesty requires the utmost discretion on this."

Ember nodded, though she wanted to know that she wasn't going to be treading on anyone's toes. "Is there anything else you can tell me?"

"This is all we know at this stage, but if we have any other news I will let you know."

Ember stood, keen to get out of the palace. "Thank you, Mr Beresford. I look forward to hearing from you."

Beresford rose quickly as she left her chair and Ember smiled, unused to such a display of manners. "Miss Merrington," he called.

She turned back to him as she reached the door, waiting for him to speak.

"Sometimes," he paused, as if trying to find the right words, "things aren't quite what they seem in this city."

Ember drew herself up. "I grew up in this city, I am sure I can handle myself."

He didn't bother to hide his frown. "Just be careful," he said after a pause, handing her a slip of paper with an address on it. "I can more often be found at home. If you need anything please let me know, and please call me Daniel."

Ember took the piece of paper from him, noticing how worn her only pair of gloves were. She coloured slightly and said deliberately, "Thank you, Mr Beresford."

He let out an almost imperceptible sigh and opened the door for her, bowing slightly. "Miss Merrington."

She inclined her head and passed through the door to the footman who was lurking outside, waiting to escort her out.

❖

Ember pulled her coat tighter around herself as she crossed the road outside the palace. She was sure the fog got thicker as she drew further away from the gates, as if the palace had its own bubble of clean air. She only just made it to the pavement when a tram swished by, narrowly missing her. She felt sorry for horses who coughed and spluttered in the yellow grey miasma, prone to collapsing in the street with the effort.

She briefly contemplated catching the underground railway home but the penny fare would be better spent on a loaf to go with the rest of yesterday's soup. She could endure the murky air for the walk home.

She knew the smog wasn't helping her father's illness; she hoped that this job would pay enough for her to take him to the coast. The Change of Air cure was reputed to be helpful in bringing relief to patients with tuberculosis, though she wasn't sure anything could help, but if it brought him some respite, she was willing to try.

Reaching the bookshop she unlocked the door, flipping the sign from closed to open. The area wasn't bad—there were much worse places in London. The shop had been bought when her family was more prosperous. It was a little too far from the more fashionable literary areas like Holborn to do much business, but with her father unable to work on investigation cases it was all they had right now.

The shop occupied the front half of a large terrace property. In the lower section there were two rooms, which although separated by an archway, the placement of the many bookshelves gave it an appearance of secret passages and hidden spaces. In the corner an iron spiral staircase led to an upper level where the older and rarer books were held.

A door near the counter in the main section of the shop led through to the back room serving as both parlour and kitchen. Beyond was a small scullery with a stone sink. Upstairs there was a bedroom each for herself and her father. An attic, currently used as storage and a damp cellar, completed the extent of their dwelling, apart from a small yard and a privy out the back.

Ember stood for a moment looking round the space. She loved the bookshop—it was more than her home, it was her life. She ran her fingers over the table where she'd spent many hours with her father, while he'd taught her to read. Her favourite task had been for him to call out a title of a book and she would scurry amongst the shelves seeking it out. When she sold a book she felt like she was entrusting her friends into new hands, hoping they would be cared for by their new owners just as much as she did. But in truth, the book business was not prosperous right now. She really needed this case and was pleased she had been given a chance to prove herself.

She shook herself from her reverie and went through to the parlour. Stoking the kitchen fire, she added a few more precious coals on it trying not to notice their dwindling supplies. She gave a slight sigh at the ash that needed clearing out—a constant chore—and decided she would leave it until tomorrow. She placed the pan of yesterday's leftover soup on the hot plate to heat for their supper and went up to see how her father was, wondering how she was going to keep this case a secret from him.

Chapter Two

The clang of the shop bell disturbed Ember while she was toasting some of yesterday's loaf over the fire.

It was still early, though she had been up for several hours. She had cleared the ash from the stove and reset the fire, and a kettle was on the hot plate, heating water for a cup of tea. She had swept through and dusted and was just making breakfast for her father. He seemed better today and she hoped he would feel well enough to make it downstairs.

Setting down the toast she went through to the shop, wiping her hands on her apron. She knew that it wasn't Sam from across the street as he would have called out and come straight through, but she was unprepared for the sight of the gentleman who stood before her. It took her a moment to recognise the velvet and gold brocade that made up the livery of the palace footmen. At the palace, the uniform had seemed normal, at one with the surroundings, but here in her little shop it looked rather incongruous. It didn't help that the footman looked round him with an air of distaste, like he dared not touch anything for fear of getting a speck of dust on his clothes. Ember was taken aback; the shop and the furniture might be shabby and worn but they were clean. She stood mutely for a minute staring at him. He reached inside his coat and withdrew a sheaf of papers.

"I was asked to hand you these, Miss, er—"

"Merrington," Ember blurted, recovering herself. "Miss Merrington."

The footman nodded and gave a slight bow—the smallest possible, likely to not seem rude—and proffered the papers. "From Mr Beresford. You are expecting them, I believe."

"Yes, thank you." She took the pages from him and gave them a quick glance before looking up at the footman, wondering if there was anything else. "Please tell him thank you."

"Very good, miss," the footman bowed again, more stiffly this time and left.

His manner and sneering had irked at Ember's pride. *Giving himself airs,* she thought. *At least I run my own business.* Conveniently not adding that he was better fed, better dressed and probably made more money than she did.

Ember could hear the kettle boiling so she finished setting breakfast for her father and took it up to him. Settling in at the table in the shop with her own breakfast, she didn't want to waste a minute looking at the lists. Though the table was used for customers to review the books before they purchased, Ember had spent many hours sitting there herself. Both her parents had believed she should be well educated, undertaking the role themselves, and the shop had been her schoolroom, the table her desk.

The first page of the papers was a list of Lady Fordingworth's friends, ones that Mr Beresford had said had already been contacted. She set that aside for a moment and turned to the three pages of ball attendees. She recognised a few of the names; she was not ignorant of London society even if she did not move in those circles herself. She had often read the society periodicals as a young girl, dreaming of attending a ball and dancing with a duke or whomever was the catch that season. She shifted slightly in her seat at the knowledge that it was just a young Ember who had done this. Breathing a wistful sigh, she gathered a copy of the latest *Who's Who* and the latest few editions of *The Queen* periodical and set to work looking up those she was unfamiliar with.

It was a few hours and several cups of tea later that she noticed something that caught her eye. *This can't be right.* Her finger halted next to one name—Baron Monteray. She reached for some earlier editions of *Who's Who* and copies of *The Queen*. Frowning, she scanned through them frantically looking for references. At length, she grew disheartened from the lack of finding anything useful and she put them down, a headache forming. *How can that be possible?* Although reluctant, it was clear she needed more answers from Mr Beresford.

❖

"Sammy, Sammy, are you in there?" Ember called through the open door of the workshop.

Samuel Hinton came round from behind the contraption he was working on, wiping his dirty hands on a rag. He was a tall and rather gangly young man with unruly sandy brown hair which always looked untamed. He had a pinkish complexion and a slightly small snub nose, which made him look much younger than his twenty two years. He smiled broadly at her. "Always a pleasure, Ember, but what's up?"

"Is Ron around to run an errand for me, I have a ha'penny for him."

"He'll do it for nothing, hold on." Sam went to a door at the back of the workshop that opened to a yard and called for his brother, before walking back with the young boy, his hand resting on his shoulder.

"Now Ron, Miss Ember wants you to do something for her. Do it quick and don't get lost."

Ember leant down to the scruffy boy and told him her message, getting him to repeat it back to her and the address she gave him.

"Now off with you." Sam affectionately pushed Ron in the right direction. Only after they had watched him scamper down the street did he turn to Ember, concern on his face. "Is everything all right?"

Ember gave a brief sad smile and sighed, "Things could be better, Sam."

"Is it your pa again? Is Ron going for the doctor?"

Ember shook her head, feeling guilty that she couldn't give the real reason for the errand. She disliked keeping things from Sam, but she'd signed the Official Secrets Act. "No, he is much the same." Sam, as Ember's oldest and only real friend, knew the truth of Robert Merrington's illness.

"Things are just a little tough right now, and as you can see, people aren't queuing up to read." She gestured a hand towards the bookshop across the cobbled street.

A sadness crossed Sam's face and he said softly, "I would never let you starve, you know that."

Ember sighed and looked at him. "I know, Sam, but we both know that is not the answer." Sam had proposed to her every year since her family moved into the bookshop when Ember was seven years old. They had quickly become friends and it had been a joke between them. Once, when she was seventeen and Sam eighteen, she had nearly said yes, thinking their friendship had blossomed into something more. Then they had shared a kiss and both immediately realised it had been a terrible mistake. Things had been awkward between them for a while and Ember was afraid they had ruined the easy friendship they had enjoyed before, but the next year, on her birthday as always, Sam had proposed again and the awkwardness had been broken. Their friendship was better than it had ever been.

She regarded him. "It's about time you found someone, Sam. Someone to love you, to settle down."

He gave a wry laugh. "You know I am only wedded to my machines, Em." He jerked a thumb back into the workshop. The Hinton family business was making shoes and Sam was a skilled cobbler himself, but he also loved tinkering with machinery and had always been inventing and building things. When he was fourteen, his father had cleared out the small storeroom that stood adjacent to the shoe shop that his father still ran and allowed him to turn it into a workshop—probably more to get Sam's machines out of the house than to cultivate any talent he had. It was expected that Sam would take over the shoe shop from his father one day, so Sam was pleased when Ron, his younger brother by twelve years came along— the only other child of his mother's who had survived past infancy. He could let Ron take on the family business, as Sam was sure he was going to be famous for his machines one day.

"What are you working on now?" she asked, genuinely interested. She had never been dismissive of his dreams and big ideas, apart from the odd tease that close friends could get away with. She had spent many hours in the workshop sitting with him, sometimes talking, sometimes reading, while he worked away.

Sam smiled, the corners of his golden brown eyes crinkling, clearly pleased she had asked as she hadn't spent so much time with him of late, especially while she had been caring for her father.

"Come and have a look." He held his hand out towards the workshop door to invite her to precede him in.

The workshop had a couple benches piled high with materials, metal, leatherwork, nuts and bolts. Another bench was covered in an array of glass bottles. Liquids of various colours —red, blue, yellow and green—bubbled in some which stood over naked flames, tubes running in a complicated puzzle between them. Tools hung on the walls like sentries ready for action.

The workshop floor was dominated by a large machine. It was a mass of brass tubes and cogs. In its centre was a large chamber with a tube that puffed steam slowly and a series of glass cylinders with green liquid languidly swirling about in them.

It looked a mishmash of parts even by Sam's standards. His designs were always a bit haphazard.

"What is it?" she frowned, not sure what to make of the contraption.

"It is a type of steam engine. I am trying to make it smaller so it can be used as a personal vehicle, just for a couple of people."

"That doesn't seem very exciting. Those are awful smog making contraptions."

"Ah, but once I can prove the idea I intend to use something other than steam. Carrying coal on a small scale for this would be impractical."

"Not to mention filthy," replied Ember. "So what are you going to use instead?"

"A mix of ether and—"

"Ether?" Ember exclaimed. "Isn't that dangerous?"

Sam grinned. "I have a few ideas on how to keep it safe and it is a lot cleaner and lighter than coal. We will all be zipping around these personal carriages soon, much quicker than those cumbersome steam buses."

"Lord! I think I'll stick to walking."

Sam laughed, "I will get you in one of these yet."

"You have to get it to work first," Ember teased.

"Oh ye of little faith," Sam responded, placing his hand on his chest for dramatic effect.

Ember laughed, realising it felt good to do that. She hadn't felt much like laughing for the last few months, but she could always rely on Sam to cheer her up, something she was grateful for. She regretted that she hadn't made time for her friend enough recently.

Leaving Sam with the promise to visit again soon, she turned across the street to the bookstore. When she had left, her father was getting dressed and she had encouraged him to spend some time downstairs today. The fire was burning brightly in the kitchen and she had drawn his favourite chair up in front of it. Some days were easier than others for him, and sometimes he could even manage a walk outside. If the smog wasn't too bad tomorrow, she would suggest it. Her heart felt a bit lighter—her father was going through a good stage and she had a job, an investigation once Beresford cleared up a few facts, and wasn't that the sun she could vaguely see shining through the haze making the day seem brighter and full of possibility. Ember smiled to herself as she closed the door to the shop behind her, grateful for some small mercies.

Chapter Three

Dusk was falling when Ember decided to close up for the evening. There had been a couple of customers over the course of the afternoon, but no one for the last few hours. Still it had allowed her to give the shelves a dust and make a stew for supper with some meat she had managed to get cheaply earlier. She'd managed to save some coins it was on the turn, but that didn't matter so much in a stew.

She turned at the noise of the bell and was surprised to see Daniel Beresford standing just inside the doorway, dressed in his usual smart clothes and leaning on a cane. She had expected him to send a message of where she could meet him, not turn up at the shop.

She quickly crossed to the door to the parlour and shut it. She didn't want her father— who was dozing in his chair in front of the fire—finding out Daniel was here. Now that he was here though, she needed to ask her question and get him to leave as soon as possible. She lifted her chin and squared her shoulders, taking a deep breath.

"Mr Beresford," she started, about to continue when he spoke first.

"Miss Merrington, I am sorry I couldn't come sooner, I had a few things to attend to."

Ember frowned, certain she had not asked him to visit. Still she would not be rude. "There was no hurry."

"But the boy ..."

"Ah, Ron does have a flair for the dramatic. There was no need to come all this way, but thank you." Ember smiled graciously. "I do have a few questions. Please sit, Mr Beresford."

Ember indicated to the chairs at the study table. Daniel looked alarmed and then a little embarrassed, until Ember understood his problem with maintaining social propriety. She moved to the table and sat down. Raising her eyebrows she asked, "Is that better?"

With visible relief, Daniel sat down. Ember noticed that he was rubbing his leg, as if easing out some hurt.

"I have found something of interest," she began, remembering she had left the lists on the shop counter and rose to get them. Daniel immediately jumped up.

"Please drop the chivalry act, Mr Beresford," Ember sighed slightly. "It is all the same to me whether you sit or stand, but you don't look like you should be jumping up and down every two minutes." She glanced at his leg.

Daniel sat down again and let out a breath. "Thank you. It does still cause me pain, some days more than others." He rubbed his leg again and Ember wondered if it wasn't an unconscious habit. "What did you want to ask?"

"I have found something odd in the records of the ball guests," she started, gesturing to the retrieved lists.

Just then there was a call from the parlour. "Who is that?"

Ember froze. She thought she had been quiet, but obviously her father had woken up. She took a deep breath, briefly considering if it was rude to shove Daniel out the door.

"Em, is everything all right?" her father called again. *Well it was too late now.*

Daniel looked at Ember. "Is that your father? May I say hello? It has been many years and I would like to renew the acquaintance, if possible."

Ember sighed and indicated for him to go through. She sat staring at but not seeing the documents in front of her as she rubbed her palms down her skirt, her hands slick with sweat. Her mind was a whirl of what she was going to say to her father, to Daniel. Maybe she should apologise for concealing the extent of her father's condition, but no, she really needed this job and she was more than capable of handling it on her own.

She was just thinking she ought to perhaps go through to the parlour and put the kettle on to boil when Daniel reappeared in the doorway.

Ember looked up and saw anger flushing his face.

"Why didn't you tell me how bad he was?" Daniel spat. "You lied to us."

Ember rose from the table, and fixing Daniel with a stare, she pushed past him and closed the door so her father would not hear before turning on him.

"Would the Queen—would you—have given me this job had I told the truth?" She stared him down.

He had the decency to look away first. "No," he sighed, "probably not."

"I need this job, Daniel." He looked at her, clearly surprised at the use of his first name. "Look around you. My father cannot work. I manage to occasionally get some investigation work, mostly by wealthy women who wish to divorce their husbands and need evidence." She smiled grimly at that. "But there aren't enough clients who will trust their cases to a woman and the shop doesn't make much money," she said, gesturing to the shelves of books before continuing. "I bought the meat for tonight's supper because I sold two books today. It is the first bit of meat we have had this week, and if I don't sell any books tomorrow, we won't get any more. All I really want," she rubbed her forehead, a headache forming, "is to take my father to the coast, to get him out of this smog, and give him some clean air. But right now I can't afford the train tickets, and this job is my chance to do that for him." She stared at him, challenging him to say something, to take away her dreams now that he knew the truth.

Daniel replied, sorrow and shame crossing his face, "I'm sorry, I had no idea."

"You won't take this job away from me?" Ember asked tentatively.

Daniel paused and glanced round the bookshop, taking it in before releasing a sigh. "No, and I will not tell Her Majesty the truth about your father, not until you have had a chance to prove yourself anyway."

Ember breathed a sigh of relief. "Good, thank you."She straightened, willing herself to move on instead of letting Daniel see how much his response had affected her. "Now, I have some questions as I don't think I am the only one who has been withholding information."

Daniel frowned and moved over to the table where the pages were laid out. "What is it?"

Ember pointed to the lists. "I was cross referencing the names, all these nobles and the like, and here"—she stabbed her finger onto one name—"this must be an error."

"How so?" Daniel looked at the name.

"Because if this is correct, I cannot find a reference to

Baron Monteray. I checked back in older books but according to those, this baron is 237 years old."

"Ah." Daniel paled.

"Do you want to explain?" Ember stood back crossing her arms.

Daniel glanced towards the door leading to the back room. "You said your father had trained you." Ember nodded her assent. "Did he take you on any missions for the Crown or tell you about them?"

It was Ember's turn to drop her gaze, another half truth she had told "No, he never spoke of them."

Daniel hummed an approval "Quite right too. He has signed the documents to keep those a secret, the same as you have done."

"But you can tell me what this is about?" Ember asked.

Daniel gestured to the study table, "You might want to sit down."

Ember briefly looked at the chairs but then remembered she was going to make some tea, and if this was going to be a long or harrowing tale, she needed something to fortify her. "I would like to check on my father first. Would you like some tea?"

Just like a spell had been broken, Daniel looked older and a bit greyer. "Yes, please," he replied before sinking into one of the chairs.

Ember found her father dozing again in his chair. She knew the days ahead would be challenging—starting with whatever Daniel needed to tell her—but it would be worth it to see her father regain some of his strength. Stoking the fire, she boiled the kettle. Leaving him a tea for when he woke up, she took a tray through to the shop.

After she had poured them both a cup, she sat down and

looked expectantly at Daniel. "You were going to explain how someone could be over 200 years old," she prompted.

Daniel took a sip of his tea before drawing a deep breath. "It's more than that," he explained. "Among us there are other beings, ones which are not quite human. Things that have been on this planet much longer than we have. They are born in the shadows. We know them as demons, shapeshifters, witches—"

"You expect me to believe this?" Ember asked, her voice raising in incredulity. Clearly Daniel was unhinged—there were no such creatures, not in real life, not outside of books. She regretted asking him for help now. Maybe she should have carried on alone.

"There are many creatures beside us humans, Ember," Daniel replied patiently, unaffected by her outburst.

"Those are fairy tales told to scare children."

"Did you ever wonder how those fairy tales came about?" Ember shook her head, her brow creased.

At the sound of laboured coughing they both looked to the door. Ember's father, Robert, stood leaning on the threshold.

"It's true," he rasped, then at Daniel, "this explains why you are here. I don't want my daughter mixed up in this." A look of sadness etched in his face, he continued, "I have tried to keep this from her. It is not the future her mother would have wanted, nor I want for her."

At the mention of her mother, Ember looked at her father. "Mama knew this too?" Her voice trembled. This couldn't be true, her mother would never have kept secrets from her. Robert, maintaining eye contact with Daniel, simply replied, "Yes, she knew."

"I don't believe this, I am just looking for a missing person," Ember said, unwilling to allow any other version of her world than the one she knew.

"It is true," said Robert, "and if demons are involved, I don't want you to have any part of it."

Ember drew herself up a little bit straighter. "I have already promised the queen." She gulped, remembering that she hadn't understood what the case entailed, but she was determined to see it through. "We need the money, Papa. We need to buy coal and food, and the doctor said some sea air would help you." She smiled faintly at him. "Let me do this for you."

Robert turned to look at her. He rarely lost his temper with her, but he looked that way now. Not just angry, but frightened. "It is too dangerous, Em. You could get—will get—hurt, killed even." The last choked out as a sob. "Ask Daniel why he now walks with a limp and he is a man, not a slip of a girl."

Ember's eyes flashed. Her father in his fear had said exactly the wrong thing.

"I am old enough to make up my own mind and if you think that I am inferior just because I am a woman—"

"As stubborn as your mother," Robert interjected. "But no, Em, I will not allow it."

"I am not breaking my promise to the queen. It is just a missing person's case, we don't even know if this baron is involved. A young woman is missing, Pa, just like me. Think of her family ..."

Robert sighed resignedly. "Just this once then, and you"— he directed at Daniel, pointing at him to make sure he understood—"you will train her, and if anything happens to her, I will hold you personally responsible." This set off another bout of coughing, sending Robert back to the parlour to sit down. Ember jumped up and went to see if he needed anything. Neither of them noticed how pale Daniel had gone or how he gulped his tea down.

Returning a few minutes later, Ember asked, "I don't really

understand what this has to do with our missing Lady La-di-da."

"Not all of the things that come from the otherworld are grotesque. Some of them look just like you and me and can integrate into our society, sometimes into the upper classes."

"Do you think the baron could be a demon or something? Which I still don't believe in, despite what you and Papa say. I'm sure I would have noticed any demons."

"Do you want me to show you one?"

"What, now?" Ember was startled, did he have one hidden somewhere, in a dungeon perhaps. Ember shook her head. Now she was being ridiculous.

"Are you ready for a little training?"

"Um, okay, fine." Ember wasn't fine but she needed to have answers.

"Then get your coat. Let's see how much talent you have inherited."

"Talent? What talent?" This sounded even more incredulous than the existence of demons. "Inherited? From my father?" Ember asked.

Daniel paused for a long moment before he replied, "Yes, from your father."

❖

Daniel suggested they take the District Underground line close to the river and cross Lambeth bridge to the south side of the river. When they emerged from the Underground it was fully dark, and the smog was a little less dense near the water but it still created an atmosphere of menace that had Ember shivering. She had never feared the city before, but she wasn't sure what to expect now.

"We will not go far into the places dreachen are known to frequent," Daniel said.

"Dreachen?" Ember was sure she had heard that word before, but the memory was so fleeting she couldn't hold onto it before it slipped from her grasp.

"It is the name given to the demons and other dark things," Daniel explained. "I believe the origin is somewhere in Germany, near the Black Forest."

"Do you mean to say that there are these dreachen all over the world?" Ember asked, waving her hand to indicate that she still thought them a myth of childish stories.

"Yes. Where there are humans, you will find dreachen."

❖

They walked slowly along the embankment that followed the south side of the river. Iron railings bordered the river on one side of the wide pavement, while lamp standards, their bases adorned with dolphins, rose at intervals, the light accentuating the darkness. On the other side, a roadway, crisscrossed with tram tracks, met a range of buildings. Old wharves and warehouses rubbed shoulders with newer residential townhouses, a sign of the bustling and growing city.

"I am a Drechen hunter, as is your father," Daniel explained.

"My father is a hunter?" This sounded even more incredulous than the existence of demons. How could she have not known this? Though it would go some way to explaining the secret missions and the black chest of odd weapons. "How do you become a hunter?" Ember asked, her mind still trying to make sense of it all.

"You don't become one, you are born one, the same way

you are born with blue eyes or brown hair. Those who hunt them are able to sense Dreachen."

Ember's mind whirred. "And this is the talent as you call it, that I may have inherited from my father?" Ember huffed, "It sounds more like a curse."

"Yes, it is an inherited talent and sometimes it can be a curse. Can you feel anything?" Daniel asked her.

"I don't believe this." She shivered again, Reluctantly she scanned herself, trying to heighten the awareness of her senses, yet she felt nothing, except a sense of foolishness for something that wasn't real. "What am I supposed to feel?"

"It is different for every hunter, but for me it is a sense of foreboding."

"What about for my father?" Ember asked.

"I don't know. Like I said, it varies."

He stopped abruptly and turned to face her, placing one arm on her shoulder. "I can feel something. Now just close your eyes and don't worry, we are in the open and nothing can happen here."

Ember tentatively flickered her eyes shut and then opened them again before closing them once more.

"Now take some deep breaths and try to empty your mind."

Ember tried breathing deeply, but her mind was flitting round. "I can't feel anything," she said impatiently.

"That's okay, it might take some time. Try to focus on your breathing, count with me. Breathe in one, two, three, and out one, two, three. In one, two, three, and out one, two, three." Ember did as he said, but still struggled to shake the feelings of foolishness. "Good, now become aware of your other senses and anything else you might feel," Daniel instructed.

Ember tried again to reach into herself, but she couldn't smell anything past the pervading stench of the river. She tuned into the noises around her, but could perceive nothing out of the ordinary. She felt the tears of frustration stinging her eyes behind her closed eyelids, and she blinked them open. A wave of hopelessness washed over her. "I can't do this," Ember almost cried. "This is stupid."

Daniel let go of her shoulder and turned away. "Maybe your father is right, this is a bad idea. If you don't believe, then you won't be able to do it anyway. I will find someone else to take this case."

Panic threatened to overwhelm Ember— she couldn't afford to lose this opportunity. She tried to control her racing heart at the thought that this might be over before she'd even had a chance to prove herself. She couldn't fail, there was too much at stake."No, I need to do this." Ember caught up with him, "You promised that you would let me do this job. It's just … it just sounds a bit unreal."

"Have a rest and we will try again when you are calmer," Daniel replied. His grim look spurred Ember's need for some reassurance.

"So you won't find anyone else?" Ember held her breath, hoping she would be given another chance.

"No. Not yet anyway." She understood it was the best she was going to get right now.

As they continued walking, Ember asked, "What happened when you hurt your leg?"

Daniel looked grave and stopped by the railings to the river for a minute, taking a long time to answer. "It was the last job I did with your father, when you were just a young child. We were trying to eliminate a nest of demons, and things went wrong, horribly wrong. I was bitten by a serpentine demon, and we only just managed to get out alive. I was wounded badly and had to spend a long time convalescing. I was lucky not to lose my leg, and it was months before I could walk again. As soon as I could be moved, I was sent abroad to another part of the Empire. I have only been back in England for a few months."

Ember remained quiet for a moment, trying to picture the dangers he had faced—the same ones she could very well face. "How did you start working for the queen?" Ember asked curiously.

"I've never really stopped, but after my accident, it was clear I couldn't fight anymore. I took up an advisory position for Her Majesty, but she recalled me to help with the growing problem in London." He stood silent in his own thoughts for a minute, looking out across the river before turning back to the street. "Come, we have work to do."

The streets of London were never quiet, whatever the time of day, but as they walked further the press of people thinned and Ember practised a few deep breaths. She looked up and saw a gentleman walking up the street. He was well dressed and sported a top hat and a cloak, but she felt there was something different about him—a sense of power, but at the same time she couldn't quite focus on him.

She grabbed Daniel's arm to stop him from walking. "There," she said quietly. "There is something about the gentleman coming this way."

Daniel smiled. "Well done. In another couple of steps I was going to ask if you felt anything."

Relief flooded through her. She couldn't have explained what she felt, but something had prickled at her senses.

Daniel drew her closer to the river and turned them so they were looking away from the figure as he walked past.

"Who is he?" asked Ember.

"I do not know," said Daniel pensively as they watched the gentleman walk up the street and disappear into the gloom. "He is a very powerful demon though."

"Why did we turn away from him?" Ember asked, perplexed by Daniel's actions..

"Because sometimes they can sense us too," Daniel replied. "I don't know how it is for them all, but for some dreachen, when they look directly at us, they can see we are hunters."

Ember swallowed, trying to take in everything she had learned in the last few hours. It was hard enough to come to terms with other races, but that her father had been involved in hunting them and she might have the ability to do so as well was overwhelming. Exhaustion caught up with her and she stifled a yawn.

"I think we should get back," said Daniel, seeing her efforts to not appear weary. "We will try again tomorrow. In the meantime, spend some time practising. The breathing might seem easy, but it is a technique you need to master, then try to ground yourself before trying to sense something."

Although Ember sensed nothing more on the way back, Daniel pointed out several figures in the crowd who he said were Dreachen.

"I am still not sure about them, but are they so bad?" asked Ember. "You said most of them look like us. What about the ones who don't, what do they look like?"

"Let's hope you never have to find out."

Chapter Four

Ember opened the shop and spent a few minutes enjoying the spring sunshine on her face. Looking up and down the lane, everything seemed normal and in the daylight, she could hardly believe everything she'd learned last night. She had spent some time before getting up trying the breathing techniques that Daniel had taught her. She wasn't sure if she had been imagining it or not, but it had seemed a little easier. Sam walking across from his workshop caught her attention, a concerned look upon his face.

"Is everything okay, Sammy?" Ember asked as she ushered him into the shop.

"It's fine, though I was wondering if you were okay. The lights were on in the shop late last night," Sam said, his brows knitting in concern.

"An old friend of my father's visited, and they were reminiscing about old times," she explained before catching sight of Daniel just before he pushed open the door. "Ah, here he is now. Mr Beresford," she greeted before Daniel had a chance to say anything. "My father is just through there in the kitchen."

When Daniel's response never came, Ember realised he was looking at Sam. "This is my friend and neighbour, Samuel Hinton. His father owns the cobblers across the street."

Daniel finally looked at her, but seemed a little flustered. "Yes, of course. Good morning, Miss Merrington." He turned back to Sam and gave a small polite bow. "Pleased to meet you, Mr Hinton."

Content that introductions were out of the way, Ember pushed Sam towards the door and waved Daniel through to the kitchen.

Once outside, Sam looked mortified. "I just stood there like an oaf."

Ember frowned, "What are you talking about, Sam?"

"I just stood there like a boy from the gutter." He ran his hands through his unruly hair, his face flushed.

"I would hardly call you that." Ember replied, confused by Sam's reaction. "But what does it matter?"

"He was a gentleman, and it is his type I need to impress, and yet when I get introduced, I stand there like a tongue-tied maiden."

Ember rounded on him. "Firstly, I will have none of your nonsense about tongue-tied maidens—we are quite capable of speaking our minds. And secondly, what do mean 'impress gentlemen?'"

Sam looked away, not meeting her eyes. "If I want to get my inventions built, I need money and for that I need investors. But how can I do that if I can't even speak to the type of people I want to invest in me?" he groaned.

"I hardly think Mr Beresford has that kind of money just because he dresses well." Ember wasn't sure about this, but that didn't stop her answering. "But I do see your point. I will help you get investors, Sam, you know that." Then a thought struck her. "Does this mean you have made progress?"

The light returned to Sam's eyes and he grabbed her hand, tugging her across the street. "Yes, that is what I came to tell you. I was up most of the night. Come and have a look."

Ember let herself be chivvied into the workshop and saw the source of Sam's excitement. She agreed the contraption did look more complete. Though still a strange beast, it was more assembled than the previous day.

Sam handed her some goggles before placing his own over his eyes. He grinned as he pushed some knobs, operated various levers, and turned a couple of wheels. Suddenly the machine made a noise and shuddered with a roar, causing Ember to jump back, before it settled into just a growl.

"Doesn't that sound magnificent?" shouted Sam.

Ember was still clueless but she shouted an encouraging yes back. Then the machine did a skip and belched out a cloud of black smoke that filled the workshop. They both started coughing and Ember pushed the door open desperate to get into some clearer air, at least what could pass as clear in London. Sam followed her outside, still coughing. "I think I need to adjust the mixture," he explained.

"I think you might," laughed Ember, handing back her goggles. "Anyway, I need to see to my pa. I am sure he and Mr Beresford will be wanting a cup of tea by now," she said, but Sam had turned back to the workshop, already focussed on fixing his machine.

Ember smiled to herself as she headed back to the shop.

❖

Robert and Daniel were deep in conversation when Ember entered the kitchen. She thought her father looked better, and having Daniel visit appeared to be beneficial to him. She let them talk while she made some tea and after pouring them a cup, she took hers into the shop where she noticed a couple of unfamiliar books on the table. She found all books interesting, but these seemed to promise something out of the ordinary. She reached out to touch one. *It couldn't hurt to take a look.* As her fingers brushed the cover, she heard footsteps crossing the kitchen and she jumped back, not wishing to be caught snooping.

Daniel appeared in the doorway and Ember smiled at him, hoping her previous panic didn't show. "I think you are doing my father some good."

Daniel glanced back at the kitchen before replying, "It is good to see him after so long, but I don't want to tire him too much and we have work to do."

Ember was pleased that her father enjoyed Daniel's company and he seemed to enjoy it too, which made her curious. "Why did you lose touch?" she asked.

Daniel shook his head slightly, his smile fading. "As I said yesterday, I was sent abroad, and it was too long ago to worry about now."Crossing to the table he sat down, clearly not willing to elaborate on the matter.

"Has there been any advancement in the case?" he asked.

Ember looked back at the lists on the table. "Well, Lady what's-her-face—"

"Lady Margaret Berthilda Fordingworth," corrected Daniel.

Ember waved her hand in a gesture which clearly meant whatever and continued, "Has been missing for four days now, and we are running out of time. I want to visit some of her friends. I will start with …" Ember ran her finger down the page, stopping next to one name. "Harriet Belvedere, she seems to have been her closest friend."

Daniel nodded approvingly before pushing the peculiar

books towards her. "I have brought you these as I think they might help."

The books were bound in embossed leather, well worn and used.

"What are they?" Ember asked, picking up a slim volume. Opening the book, she flicked through a few pages of hand-written notes and ink drawn pictures.

She turned to the front and read *Thoughts on Demons and Other Creatures by Aloysius Harper, Daemorgtarga 1721–1778.*

"Daemorgtarga," she whispered to herself, wondering why it sounded familiar, the veils of her memory just shimmering out of reach.

"What is this word?" she pointed, showing Daniel.

"Demon hunter. Daemorg is demon, Targa is hunter."

Ember's finger traced the word again. "Are they journals?"

"No printed works exist of the dreachen, to what printer could we trust such information. All knowledge has to be passed down through hunters or their journals."

She considered his words, her gaze narrowing at the stack of books. "How did you get them?"

Daniel looked away, running a hand over his face and briefly pinching the bridge of his nose before taking a breath and answering, "I am known as a collector amongst other hunters, so if one sadly passes, or is killed, their journals tend to find their way to me."

Ember swallowed before picking up another tome, beginning to understand the legacy of information it held. This one looked even older and the script was difficult to read.

"The information held here is useful, but just a fraction of what we should know. What we really need is the Codex," Daniel explained, a hint of frustration seeping into his voice.

"The Codex?"

"The Dreachen Codex is the oldest and most definitive

work on all types of demons, shifters and witches, both in general terms and specific powerful individuals. It spans generations of hunters."

Ember was curious, and as a booklover and seller, the thought of such a book was exciting. "That sounds really interesting. I would love to see it."

"It is lost." They both turned to see Robert standing in the doorway.

"Lost?" Ember asked, trying not to sound disappointed.

Robert shrugged, "Maybe in the move here, but I haven't seen it in years."

"Pa, *you* had the Codex?" Ember stared at her father in disbelief, trying to come to terms with yet another secret that had been hidden from her.

"Not anymore," he replied flatly.

"You have looked for it?" Daniel asked.

"Of course I have," Robert replied angrily before turning back to the kitchen and slamming the door behind him.

Daniel stared at the door for a long moment, his mouth a grim line, before turning back to Ember. "Have you seen an unusual book?" he asked. "It is large and thick and very old."

"No, and I have spent years immersed in these shelves. We don't have anything like that, I would have noticed." Ember frowned. "But I can't believe my father would have lost it."

"Nor me," murmured Daniel.

Chapter Five

E mber checked the address again on the note and looked up at the house before her. It was a large four-storey terrace in Fitzrovia, bordering the fashionable Bloomsbury. She adjusted her hat and smoothed down her coat and skirt. Taking a deep breath, she walked up to the front door and rang the bell.

A maid answered and looked at her, and for a moment Ember worried she was going to tell her that the tradesperson's entrance was round the back, or that they didn't need whatever she was selling, so she decided to speak first.

"Please, I wish to see Miss Belvedere."

The maid sniffed and held out her hand for a card. Ember didn't have visiting cards of her own—those were for ladies who had nothing to do all day but call on each other—but she was prepared for this and used one of the bookshop's cards. She handed one to the maid with *I wish to speak to you about Lady Margaret, from a friend* written on the back.

The door was shut on her and she had nothing to do but wait. She turned round and viewed the other houses on the street. The road was wide and planted with cherry blossom trees, which were now showing their pink blooms in the spring sunshine. At length the door opened again and Ember turned back to find the maid holding it open for her. "Miss Belvedere will see you for a few minutes."

She was shown into the first room to the right of the door, a large handsome room covered in blue wallpaper. Blue was a pervading theme with couches and cushions decked out in the colour. There were predominantly blue paintings on the wall and a Turkish carpet on the floor. Ember thought it was a bit overpowering to the senses, but then she wasn't used to seeing so much colour in one room at once.

She didn't have long to wait before a young lady came in and shut the door behind her. She was thin, her dark green day dress making her pale skin look almost translucent. She had large brown eyes and dark hair which was drawn up on her head.

"Miss Belvedere?" Ember queried. The lady looked a little nervous but crossed the room to Ember.

"Yes, what do you know of Lady Margaret?" she asked quickly. "Oh apologies, I haven't even asked who you are. It is just such a horrible affair."

Ember took note of the lady's dark eyes darting about, and the way she seemed to exude nervous energy. "Forgive me," she said, "I am Miss Merrington. I am an investigator".

"Oh really, how exciting!" Harriet's eyes lit up for a moment.

Ember continued, "I have been asked to look into the disappearance of Lady Margaret."

"Ha, I knew you weren't a friend, though your note said you were. A true friend would know that she likes to be called Tilda." Ember's eyebrows shot up and Harriet slapped a hand across her mouth "Oh lord, I do talk too much. Mama is always telling me off for it."

The use of a nickname gave Ember hope that Miss Belvedere would be in a position to provide more information. "Is there anything you can tell me about her disappearance?" asked Ember gently.

"Her father has already asked me," said Harriet. "Though I didn't tell him anything, I was too upset. Oh, I do hope she is all right." She began twisting a handkerchief in her hands.

"Do you know if she was planning to meet anyone on the night of the Hamilton's Ball?" asked Ember.

"Well," began Harriet, "you never know with Tilda. She is such a daredevil, but I do know she had received a note the day before the ball."

"A note? From whom?" asked Ember.

"I think it was from Baron Monteray," Harriet said thoughtfully.

"The baron!" exclaimed Ember. If what Daniel suggested was true about the baron, this was becoming a very interesting case. She suspected he was involved somehow, but having it confirmed gave her greater concern over Lady Margaret's safety. "But you didn't tell that to her family?"

"Oh no, I didn't want to get Tilda into trouble or the baron —he is so charming." Harriet had a slightly dreamy expression on her face that Ember tried to ignore. "Tilda is so lucky to have his attention. But he is a gentleman—he wouldn't have done anything to harm her, would he?"

"I hope not," replied Ember, trying to keep the exasperation from her voice. "Do you know what the note said?'

Harriet frowned then. "Tilda showed it to me, but it was rather odd. I thought it might be a token of love, but all it said was *You will be able to help me more than you know.* How odd is that?"

Ember agreed it was rather peculiar. "What makes you think it was from the baron?"

"That's who Tilda thought it was from. She had received a note previously which appeared to come from him and they were seen walking together at the Carrington's house a couple of weeks ago. They were taking a turn round the rose garden."

"I see," answered Ember, trying to put the pieces together. "But you don't think the baron is behind her disappearance?"

"Oh no!" Miss Belvedere gasped, clearly appalled at the accusation. "If they were planning something, wouldn't they have eloped or gone away? But the baron is still in town. Miss Carrington says her brother goes to the same club and he is often in there with his friend Mr Ashton," Harriet reasoned with herself. "And I have heard he is to give a ball himself this weekend."

"Is he? That is interesting." Ember tucked away this information to think about later and tried a different approach. "Does Lady Margaret have any enemies?"

"No, not Tilda ..." Harriett thought for a minute. "Though she doesn't really get on with Miss Ashton."

"Miss Ashton?"

Harriet's eyes darkened. "She is a b—" Again she slapped her hand across her mouth then went on to say, "Sorry, Mama says I will get into trouble if I don't learn to think before I speak. I don't care much for Miss Ashton myself, but I did hear she had set her sights on the baron."

Ember paused, processing this information. All the leads seemed to be heading back to the baron, And she was curious to find the connection. "Do you think she is behind the disappearance of Lady Margaret?"

"I don't know," said Harriet, "but I don't trust her."

"Have you heard anything at all from Lady Margaret or any of her other friends?"

"No, sorry." Harriet replied softly, looking close to tears. "It is just so awful,"

Seeing her tears, Ember realised there was nothing more Harriet could tell her and pulled on her gloves. "Thank you, Miss Belvedere. You have been most helpful."

"You will find Tilda, won't you?" Harriet placed a hand on Ember's arm, her grip surprisingly firm as she blinked away her tears and gave Ember a determined look.

Ember covered Harriet's hand with her own and gave her what she hoped was a reassuring smile. "I will do my best."

Chapter Six

Ember sat with her feet curled under her in a chair near the fire in the parlour. They had just finished supper and she was having a few moments' rest before getting up. Supper had been surprisingly successful. Ember had spied a hot potato seller on the way back to the shop and bought some for them. Daniel had showed up with some cold meats, which Ember was grateful for, and her father, seeing that Daniel was joining them, had given Ember a few pennies and sent her out to get a jug of small beer from the local tavern for them to enjoy. This made a nice change from tea. Her father and Daniel had been reminiscing and Ember had enjoyed listening to them. At length she unfurled her legs, stretched and stood up. Collecting the plates, she placed them in the stone sink in the scullery and headed into the shop. She had something she wanted to do before her next training session with Daniel.

"*Ashton, Ashton,*" she muttered to herself as she ran her finger down the list of names. Ah yes, there he was. He hadn't stood out as anything out of the ordinary when she had first looked. She pulled the copy of *Who's Who* closer and started flicking through the pages. She frowned—here it said he was twenty-eight years old. Not 200 years old like Monteray supposedly was. *What is going on?* she thought.

An idea flashed in her mind and she reached for the society magazine, *The Queen*. Harriet had mentioned *Miss* Ashton—Ashton had a sister. She looked through a few more periodicals and found her—Lady Severina Ashton—in an article about the latest fashions. She was just musing on whether there was a link in that information when Daniel came through from the kitchen.

She hadn't had time to talk to him when he had arrived and was eager to share what she'd learned.

"Do you know where Baron Monteray lives?"

Daniel stopped in the middle of the room, his lips pressed together in a slight grimace. "Please don't do anything stupid."

Ember gave him her most withering look. "I have done a fair amount of spying, usually on errant husbands—I think I can be discreet. I won't approach him, I just want to see what he looks like."

Daniel looked away for a moment, chewing his lip before he sighed and nodded. "I will send you his address tomorrow, but right now we have some training to do. Have you been practising your breathing and grounding techniques?"

Ember groaned, "Yes, but it's not doing any good."

Daniel let out a rare chuckle. "It takes months, sometimes years, to master this."

Ember huffed a reply as she shrugged on her coat. "I don't have *months*, I have days at best."

"Well, we had better get practising then," Daniel said as he held the door open for her. Ember gave him a stony look as she passed through.

❖

As they headed down the street, Ember noticed the door to Sam's workshop was open, light spilling out onto the cobbles. She poked her head round the door as a quick greeting, just to tell him she was going out again for a short while, and received a vague wave in reply.

She joined Daniel back on the lane and they started walking at a pace his limp would allow.

Daniel glanced back at the workshop. "A close friend is he?"

"I've known him most of my life," replied Ember.

"And you are not …"

"If you are asking if we are romantically involved, then no, we are not, but it would be none of your business if we were." Ember flashed at him, angry at his impertinence.

"What we do is a dangerous business," Daniel sighed. "I am sorry for prying, but I was going to suggest that if you were attached, he should at least know your work may put you in harm's way."

Ember gave a rueful smile. "I see, but no, we are just best friends. And besides, the only thing Sammy cares about is his inventions."

Daniel cocked his head in interest. "Inventions?"

"Oh yes," Ember replied. "He is currently designing a vehicle that runs on ether."

Daniel raised his eyebrows. "Is he now?" he mused, then continued walking, wrapped up in his own thoughts for a while.

Ember noticed they were taking a different route from what they had the previous night. South of the river, they headed east towards Bermondsey. Ember was used to seeing slums or rookeries, so called because they housed lots of families, often in single rooms. The buildings towered above the street several storeys high, set round central courtyards that Ember wouldn't want to wander into. But here it was different, worse even. The buildings were ramshackle and the proximity to the river, combined with the low land level, gave the area a permanent dampness, which flooded in the winter months. There were people everywhere, leaning out of windows, calling across the sodden lanes at each other—a cacophony of speech, shouts and wails. People leant against doorways and on street corners. It was a miasma of humanity.

"Where are we?" asked Ember, looking round her and pulling her coat tighter as if for protection. It wasn't a place she would want to be, even in daylight, but after dark it was even more sinister. She stepped over an overflowing open sewer that wound its way through the street.

"This is Jacob's Island," Daniel explained. "It is a good place for the dreachen to hide. In a large crowd of people they are less likely to be noticed, and it is so busy here that it is easy to hide in plain sight."

They walked further on, past the slums and across a wasteland, towards some warehouses and other businesses. They soon left the noise and bustle behind and Ember found it even more terrifying without other people around.

Daniel stopped abruptly and leant on his cane. "We are here to meet someone."

"Are we in any danger?" she asked, trying not to let her breathing speed up. Her eyes darted around her, alert to who might be appearing out of the darkness.

"Not at this moment, no," he smiled reassuringly.

Ember didn't like how temporary that sounded and asked in a hushed but worried tone, "What does that mean?"

Daniel pressed his lips together and looked away, avoiding her eyes. "There are some types of Dreachen, just a few, that we do not hunt, who we keep in our employ. Informants, if you will."

Ember couldn't believe what she was hearing but Daniel continued, "And in exchange, we turn a blind eye to what they do."

"You allow them to murder and maim innocent people?" Ember hissed. "You bring me to the middle of nowhere, in the midst of murderers, with no more protection than, than, than a lame—"

Hurt flashed across Daniel's face and Ember immediately regretted her words. She'd let fear get the better of her and lashed out. "I am sorry, Daniel. I didn't mean that." Her face red with shame and thinking he would want rid of her, she turned to go.

"Ember, wait and listen," Daniel called. "I know what I am and there's not a day that goes by that I don't wish I could change it, but please let me explain."

She paused, his acceptance of her outburst making her feel more disappointed with herself. Her cheeks still burned as she reluctantly faced him. Still wary of the situation with fists clenched by her sides, she was ready to turn and flee if needed. Her eyes continued to dart over the dark and looming buildings around her.

"These are not murderers. They do not hurt people, but they are also not like us. Demons don't just prey on humans, they prey on other demons and dreachen as well. Sometimes they stay hidden for their own safety and what they tell us helps keep them safe also," he explained, his tone serious as his grey eyes searched hers. "Please trust me, Ember. You need to learn this."

Ember slowly let out a breath and unclenched her fists.

"This is also a good place to practise," said Daniel softly. "Close your eyes and focus your breathing."

"Not a chance," answered Ember, about to turn again before Daniel caught her arm. "Are you mad? Close my eyes here?"

"It is safe," Daniel insisted. "It is a good place to practise."

Ember panicked but blew out another breath, trying to calm herself. This was the worst time ever to try these exercises. She should be doing them when already calm and relaxed, not with her heart beating so hard she could hear it. She closed her eyes, but after a couple of seconds she opened them again in frustration. "I can't do it."

"I agree this is not ideal but as you reminded me, you don't have years or even months, so this is the quickest way to learn," said Daniel. Keeping his voice soft he added, "Listen to my voice. Now close your eyes, breathe slowly in—one, two, three—and release slowly—one, two, three."

Ember followed his instructions and found that his soothing voice helped calm her. After a few minutes of listening to him, she realised her heart was no longer hammering in her chest and she felt better. Suddenly more aware of her other senses, she could pick out sounds drifting over from the rookeries and if she listened hard, she could almost identify what was being shouted. Underneath the pervading stench of poverty, she could detect an earthier, musky smell, and then, very faintly, she felt something. It was like a tingling, not in any physical way, but more like she had a barrier round her and someone was pushing against it.

"I can feel something," she whispered, not wishing to break the feeling.

"Where is it coming from?" asked Daniel quietly.

Ember focussed again. "Behind me, somewhere over my left shoulder."

"Good," Daniel said. "Can you tell how far away?"

Ember sought the tingling sensation again, trying to gauge

its distance by the intensity. After a few seconds she queried, "About twenty feet?"

"You can open your eyes now." Ember did as instructed. The street was very dark, only lit with a few gas lamps, and she still blinked a few times.

Daniel was smiling at her. "Turn around."

Ember turned and exactly where she had indicated stood an old man. He wasn't tall, his slightly hunched form adding to his diminishing figure, and he was of a slight build. His straight hair, long enough to be gathered at the nape of his neck, would have once been a glossy back, but was mostly shot through with grey, mottling his eyebrows and moustache as well. He bowed very slightly at Ember and as he raised his head to look at her, she noticed his eyes and features, marking him from somewhere in the east. *China, no, Japan,* Ember thought. She had been in the Chinese quarter of the city enough to notice he looked different. She glanced briefly at Daniel. "I don't understand."

Daniel was still smiling slightly at her but waved his hand towards the old man, who before Ember's eyes changed into a fox. He looked old in his fox form, his once vibrant orange fur sprinkled with white hairs while grey tinged his black paws and three tails.

Ember involuntarily stepped back. "It's all right," said Daniel. "He won't harm us."

"I—" began Ember, then gathering herself, "I'm not scared, it was just a surprise." She found curiosity got the better of her then and she took a few steps towards the fox, who now sat regarding her.

Daniel waved his hand again and the fox changed back into the old man, who bowed to her once more.

"This is Jannan," explained Daniel. "He is a Kitsune, a shapeshifting fox."

The old man's eyes twinkled slightly as said, "I am no murderer, miss. Not of humans anyway, but a fox has to eat you know." He gave a little shrug as a way of saying it was something he could not help. His English was impeccable, but Ember found his accent interesting and wanted to hear it again.

"Please tell me more, Mr Jannan," she asked.

"Just Jannan, if you don't mind, miss. I am from a long line of Kitsune, and I came from my native land of Japan twenty years ago. There had been a purge on our kind in my region and several of us thought we would find a better life here in the largest city in the world."

"And did you?" asked Ember.

"Let me just say we found a different life." There was a sadness to the old man's words.

"What is a Kitsune?" She was keen to know.

"Some call us demons, though I admit sometimes we can appear so, and we have been called mischievous, but we mostly serve to teach life lessons to those who need it."

"Oh," blinked Ember. That was not what she had been expecting at all. "Are there many of you?" she asked.

"In the old country, I do not know, but here there are just a few families left, and I fear that if we do not return soon, we will die out."

She felt her brows knit in confusion and Jannan explained, "Our gene pool is too small, and one of the downsides of removing ourselves from our old community is we cannot bring in fresh blood."

"Ah yes, I see your problem," she replied.

"We cannot sustain the human form for long, so we spend most of our time in our fox form."

Ember was disconcerted. She understood the dreachen to all be monsters and murderers, and yet she could feel some empathy towards the creature in front of her, one whose existence as a species was threatened. She briefly allowed herself to wonder what she could do to help him before berating herself for letting her guard down. "How do you know each other?" Ember addressed both Jannan and Daniel, eager to change the subject. It was Daniel who answered.

"When I was a young man, I was hunting a particularly dangerous type of shapeshifting demon, a shadow leopard, and I met Jannan and his family. At first I was suspicious of them as the demon I was hunting could also assume any form."

"Yes, I remember being pinned down in that alley," Jannan interjected, rubbing his chin and smiling. "You and the other gentleman were quite the pair of hunters in those days."

Daniel gave a quick grin. "With Jannan's help, I learned more of where the demon was hiding, and I was able to track and kill it. Since then, Jannan and his family have been helpful in many cases and in turn, I have tried to help them."

Ember felt her previous dismay at her emotions slowly morphing into intrigue. She had expected to be scared and to feel in danger, yet she felt kindly towards this old man. "Can I meet your family?" she asked.

"Someday, maybe, if we know we can trust you like we can Daniel san," the old man replied.

Ember nodded, understanding that trust went both ways. "Can you tell us anything about a Baron Monteray?"

Jannan shook his head. "We don't know of any barons as we do not tend to mix in the higher end of demon society."

Suddenly he stiffened and sniffed the air, turning his head over his shoulder. "Something comes, you had better go. You need to get out of here now," he said urgently before slipping back into fox form and slinking off into the shadows.

Daniel let out a curse, "Damn, I should have been paying attention."

He took hold of Ember's elbow and made to move off the street. "We need to go."

Ember couldn't move. She could feel whatever was approaching, her senses tingling in a way that was almost painful. It was either very large or extremely powerful, but for some reason she was rooted to the spot.

"Come on," urged Daniel. "We are in danger here."

Overcome by a sense of dread and foreboding, she could feel nothing but despair that seemed to suck the life force from her. Daniel brought his cane down firmly on her foot. "Ow," she exclaimed, but it had been enough to get her attention. Daniel started to drag her to the side of the street, but she shook off his hand and pushed him in front of her. He had enough of a job trying to move quickly with his limp, she didn't need to slow him down.

They reached a recessed doorway in a nearby building and pushed themselves towards the back, into the shadows. "Is this safe?" whispered Ember, unsure the recess was adequate protection from whatever was heading their way. She didn't feel ready for this and briefly regretted agreeing to train. She sank back as far as she could go, trying not to make a sound and hoping the pounding of her heart wasn't as loud as she could hear it.

"It will have to be," answered Daniel, sounding uncertain. "Just don't look directly at it."

A large hulking shape rounded the corner and started down the street.

A crushing sensation weighed on her chest and her limbs grew numb. Struggling to breathe, she tried not to gasp in air for fear of making any noise. She had felt nothing like this before it was pure terror that came in waves over her. She had never felt so helpless, so defenceless.

It looked to be a large wolf-like creature. Walking upright, it towered to roughly eight feet tall, its gait an ponderous lurch. It was a huge, bulky beast, its muscled body covered in a hairy pelt with long limbs ending in large claws. It emitted a low growl as it moved, more of a noise felt than heard. Ember caught sight of a long nose and the small amount of light given off by the gas lamps glinted off sharp teeth.

It stopped close to their hiding place, sniffing the air. Ember tried to swallow, finding her mouth had gone dry.

She pressed herself further back, squeezing her eyes shut, hoping if she couldn't see it, then it couldn't see them. She knew Daniel was also holding his breath and the seriousness of their situation nearly overwhelmed her. If something happened to them both, what would become of her father? She felt guilty that she had been so hasty to want this. Time slowed to a crawl and Ember feared she wouldn't be able to hold her breath for much longer when the pressure in her chest began to ease. She sensed the creature had moved on, though she felt she could still track where it was.

When it was out of sight, she straightened and stepped out of the doorway, gulping down air and trying to shake the tingling sensation of being tense and still for so long from her limbs. She whispered, "What was that?"

"That was a woodwolf," answered Daniel, also taking deep breaths. "A very powerful and dangerous type of dreachen." He looked shaken, scanning up and down the streets to see if it was safe. He sighed and closed his eyes briefly. "I can't sense it any more."

"Aren't those the things you are supposed to hunt?" she asked. "Not hide in doorways from?" Though she had been more than happy to hide from it.

"Look at me." Daniel's hands fisted, anger flashing in his eyes. Then he bowed his head, his voice breaking. "My dreachen hunting days are over."

Ember felt renewed shame at her earlier outburst, bitterly regretting what she had said. Daniel had been injured just doing his duty.

Now that Ember realised the real threat of the dreachen, she was curious where the hunters were. "What about others in the department then? Surely someone should be doing something about it."

Daniel ran a hand through his hair and sighed, "There is no demon hunting department anymore. It was Prince Albert who set up the department to control the dreachen, but since his death, the department has become as good as extinct. There are so few hunters left, and those who were not killed in action became too old to hunt. If there were any pressing cases, then individuals would be called upon such as your father. Her Majesty has no appetite to revive the department."

Ember felt hollow at the thought that there was no one left to protect people from the dreachen. The feeling of terror was subsiding, and she realised it was an effect the creature exuded rather than her own reaction, though she had been scared enough. But what struck her more was how powerless she had felt. She never wanted to feel like that again and she didn't want others to either. She turned to Daniel. "I want you to teach me to fight."

Chapter Seven

The next morning Ember was awake early, spending some time practising her breathing exercises and focussing her senses and awareness. She didn't know why she had frozen last night, but she felt foolish and ashamed. She rubbed the sore spot on her foot where Daniel had jabbed her with his stick.

She was concerned with his revelation that there was no one to tackle these monsters, that the department was no more. Who was protecting the people? How could the Crown idly sit by while these beasts roamed the streets? She shook her head, trying to dissipate the thoughts—it wasn't her problem to solve. She couldn't afford to get wrapped up in it all, not when her father needed her.

Daniel had at least agreed to teach her to fight. She had felt so defenceless yesterday when that thing—*what did he call it? A Woodwolf*—had passed by. Whilst she probably wouldn't have put up much of a fight if it had noticed them, she never wanted to feel so helpless again.

She had already been across to Sam's that morning and asked to borrow a pair of his trousers—she couldn't learn to fight in a skirt. He had quizzed her about the unusual request, but what could she tell him? She wasn't allowed to say anything, but knew she couldn't keep lying to him forever. They knew each other too well for secrets this large. It was a good thing that he was distracted with his machine at the moment.

Ember was in the shop when Daniel arrived. He raised his eyebrows at her attire but said nothing.

"What are we going to learn first?" she asked Daniel. He cast an eye towards the kitchen, and Ember shook her head. "Father is still in bed. I think the last few days have tired him, though I am sure he will want to see you later."

He gestured towards her attire, "I was wondering what he would say about those ..."

Ember grinned, "I can guess, but what he doesn't know won't hurt him."

Daniel smirked at her answer and then turning serious asked, "You haven't told him, have you?"

"No, and I don't intend to either, so don't you say anything," Ember warned. Daniel held up his hands in supplication. Looking around the shop he said, "There isn't much room in here. Do you have a yard?"

Flipping the shop sign to *Closed* and locking the door, Ember led him through the kitchen and scullery and out into the yard. It was small, enclosed within high brick walls, and barely larger than the shop. Daniel grunted, "This will do for today, but I think you should come to the palace. There are rooms for training and it would be easier to keep it from your father."

She was keen to get started and bounced from foot to foot with a grin, eager to get on with it. he let out a laugh at the thought of training at the palace, the notion both ridiculous and intriguing.

Daniel started by showing her some physical exercises. He had her squatting, making her stay in the same position until her legs burned, then followed up with some sit-ups. She felt she was going to vomit after doing these for a while, but these were not as bad as making her push her own body weight up on her arms. She collapsed several times before managing a couple of shaky repetitions, which were achieved more through determination than ability. More than once she wondered if she had it in her to master these exercises.

Finally he called a halt to the exercises. She stood panting, and couldn't believe that Daniel was hardly breathing any harder, despite having done the same exercises. He might walk with a limp, but he was still in good shape.

Daniel allowed her a few minutes' rest before showing her another set of movements, which were very fluid, moving from one position to another. She thought they almost felt like a dance and found them a lot easier than the more strenuous exercises.

"What are they?" Ember asked, intrigued as she had never seen anything like it before.

"I learnt them when I was overseas. They help with muscle strength, flexibility and most importantly, balance. They helped me regain some strength after my accident." Daniel's face darkened briefly before lightening again. "Let's go through them again so you can practise these when you are on your own. You can never do these too much."

Eventually, after an hour or so, he ended the lesson for the day. Ember's body felt tired and limp, though she felt exhilarated by the exercises. She hadn't realised how hard they would be.

She ran some water into the sink in the scullery and

sloshed it over her face, savouring how wonderfully cool and refreshing it felt on her skin.

"Practise the movements by yourself," Daniel repeated as she was drying her face. "The breathing exercises will also help, but you did good for your first time today." Ember felt a warmth spreading through her chest and limbs that helped mitigate some of the soreness in her muscles. She couldn't help but smile, feeling more confident in being able to solve the case.

❖

Later Ember sat cross-legged on her bed trying some of the mind-calming exercises Daniel had shown her. He explained he had learnt them when he was in India, in West Bengal. The first exercise required her to sit still and focus on her breathing, which was harder than she thought.

How can breathing be this difficult? I do it all the time. She found herself taking several deep breaths, followed by small quick ones because she felt breathless. *This can't be right.* She tried the next exercise which was to empty her mind, to welcome the silence. Daniel had explained that this would allow her other senses to heighten. She closed her eyes, still trying to breathe, trying to not to think about how hard it was, and tried to silence her mind. A flash of memory came of her sitting in this position when she was a child, but just as quick it was gone.

Every time she thought she was getting close to stillness, an unwanted thought popped into her head. How was she going to find the missing lady? Where was the Codex? Was Sammy going to invent something useful? What was she going to do about the supper she had invited Daniel to? Sighing, she gave up and went downstairs. Her father had felt well enough to stay in the shop for the first time in several weeks. This pleased her, and though she felt a stab of guilt at the thought, she was relieved that he was stronger as she would be spending more time away from the shop whilst training and solving this case. She was sure some of the improvement in her father was thanks to Daniel. He seemed to have given her father some renewed energy.

When she entered the shop, he handed her a note, a small, tired smile tugging at his lips. "This arrived half an hour ago," he explained. Breaking open the seal, she saw an address in Daniel's handwriting and whistled. It was close to Hyde Park, a very affluent part of town. Whoever this baron was, he clearly had money.

"How are you feeling, Papa?" she asked, concerned he might be exerting himself too much.

"You are asking if I can look after the shop while you go off on another errand, aren't you?" Robert gave her a small smile.

"I never could fool you," Ember replied and went to give him a quick embrace.

He waved her off, "I will be fine and if I am not, I will close up. We aren't busy at the moment anyway."

This was true—the early afternoon was their quietest time as customers usually came in the morning or early evening.

"Thanks, Papa. I will pop over and see if Sam can check on things in a bit," she said, pulling on her hat and coat.

"I'll be fine," Robert grumbled and Ember smiled at him. He was always stubborn, a trait she had inherited, but she would feel better if Sam was about. She gave her father a brief goodbye and stepped out into the weak afternoon sun.

She caught Sam bending over his machine and quickly explained what she wanted.

"You off to spy on some poor sap who hasn't realised that his wife isn't amenable to sharing him?" he asked teasingly.

"Something like that," replied Ember, ignoring the twinge of guilt at how easily the lie slipped out. "Thanks, Sam, I owe you one."

❖

Heading down the street, Ember decided to walk over to Hyde Park. Keeping awareness of her surroundings as the streets were busy as always and she didn't want to get knocked down, she tried the exercises again. She was curious if she could sense anything like the previous night. She knew it was important to master these abilities and trying to not let apprehension get the better of her, she kept her vision soft and regulated her breathing. Once she thought she felt a tingling, but when she looked round there was no one there. She shrugged and carried on.

The baron's house was one of a row of large terraced houses, with four floors above street level and one below. A wide staircase led up from the street to the main door and a smaller set of stairs led down to a basement. Built of white stone, it was four windows wide. It bordered a square which had a central park edged in ornate black railings. She entered the park area so she could observe the house without standing out on the street. Dark pink blossoms adorned cherry and plum trees and the spring sun had brought out the plump magnolia blooms. She enjoyed them for a moment. With few trees in her area of town and only having a yard behind the house and shop, a garden was a rare treat. Sighing, she returned to her task and looked back at the house. Sitting at a bench, which afforded her a view of the house but where she felt she was mostly obscured by a bush, she returned to her exercises, determined to master them.

There were a few women pushing prams along the paths in the park, nannies, Ember presumed. She received a few disapproving looks—probably because she was a young lady out without a friend or chaperone—but she ignored them and tried to look like she was waiting for someone. A young couple walked arm in arm, the woman laughing at something the gentleman had said, and he stopped to pluck her a magnolia flower. She seemed delighted with it. Ember smiled and sighed; she didn't crave love. She dared not allow herself to think of it as she saw little opportunity of it ever happening for her. Her main priority was to care for her father, and she owed him so much as he had taken care of her alone. She wouldn't entertain the thought that she could leave him. But sometimes, such as when she was watching the young couple together, she did wonder what her future held.

A movement caught her eye and she cursed herself for allowing her attention to wander away from the house. She watched as a gentleman lightly ran up the wide steps and knocked on the front door of the house. He was admitted as soon as it was opened. Ember hadn't been able to get a good look at his face as his back was to her, but had noticed he was tall and wore a brown frock coat over lighter trousers. He had also been wearing a top hat, which was perched upon golden curls, and he carried a cane, though he hadn't used it. *Was that the baron?* she thought, then decided probably not as he wouldn't have knocked on his own front door.

She sat with interest, wondering who the visitor had been. She dared not look away again. After about a quarter of an hour, the door opened and two gentlemen started down the steps. One of them was the gentleman she had seen going in earlier. His companion was easily as tall and wore a dark coat, which looked blue or even black. He had a similar top hat but atop dark hair that curled to the base of his neck. He had an angular face, which looked sharp and not one easily moved to merriment, unlike the first gentleman who had an easy countenance and was smiling now. As they reached the steps they turned and walked along the street. Once they had passed where Ember sat in the park, she rose and slowly headed to follow them. She wasn't sure if the dark haired gentleman was the baron or not, but she was interested to see where they went.

They crossed the street and headed out onto the main thoroughfare. Passing a row of shops, they entered a tobacconist, and Ember walked on past. Luckily there was a milliner's boutique two shops along the street and she stopped to look in the window while she waited for them to emerge again. When they returned, she kept her face to the window as they passed her. She dared not try to sense them and only after they passed did she realise she had been holding her breath. They were talking and she heard the one in the brown coat say, "Come, Monteray, won't you dance with my sister at the ball?" She tried to suppress a wry smile—she was correct in thinking this was the baron. In anticipation she tried to get a bit closer, her heart rate quickening.

The baron answered glumly, "You know I will, no one can hold a candle to your sister, Ashton, but I am still heartily sorry that I agreed to hold this ball for her. She caught me in a moment of weakness." Ember recognised the name from her visit to Miss Belvedere and strained to hear more.

Ashton was not put off as he grinned, "You know she wants to show off to all her society friends. She will get her hooks into you sooner or later, old chum."

The baron replied icily, "I doubt it. I will be going to Europe within the month anyway."

Ember realised that in her eagerness to hear what they were saying, she had allowed herself to get too close. She gasped and when they turned round to see who had made the noise, she spun away to look into the nearest window. Cursing herself for her error, and her bad luck that the window she was now looking at was a butchers, she hoped they hadn't noticed and stole a look from the corner of her eye to see they had resumed walking. She waited until they got almost to the next corner before she followed, trying not to speed up as they disappeared out of sight. As she rounded the corner, she saw them enter another building, and walking slowly past she saw it was the Greyminders Club. *I can't follow them there*, she thought with a sigh of frustration, and continued down the street. Deciding they were likely to be there for quite some time, she reluctantly started to head home. She reflected that although she couldn't follow them any more tonight, she had found out some important information. She could now identify the baron and he was having a ball soon. She wanted very much to know when.

Ember spent the thirty-minute walk home contemplating how the baron could look closer to thirty than the 200 years that he possibly could be. As she entered the shop she heard raised voices from the back room.

"I've told you it's lost." She had rarely heard her father angry and was curious as to why, but also worried that he might overtax himself. She paused just outside the door.

"But why would Rose—" Ember frowned. *What did Mother have to do with this?*

"Leave it, Daniel. I don't have it," her father argued, followed by a bout of coughing. Ember pushed quickly through the door and went to her father's aid, shooting Daniel a black look. A flash of remorse crossed his face as he stalked past her into the shop. Ember helped her father into a chair.

"Papa, you need to take it easy, don't let Daniel get you worked up," she gently scolded. Robert's coughing eased and he reached for her hand, giving it a squeeze. "It's fine, Em." He looked worried, leaving Ember to think it was anything but fine, but she wasn't going to tackle her father over it. She leaned down and gave him a hug. "You stay here and I'll make us a cup of tea."

"That would be welcome, love." He gave a weak smile as she released him. She left him with some tea and took a cup through for Daniel. She set his cup down on the table before taking the chair opposite.

"What was all that about? You mentioned my mother—"

"It was nothing, just something that happened long ago."

"It sure upset my father for being nothing. He has been doing so well recently, I would hate for him to have a relapse." Ember couldn't help keep the reproof from her voice. She was sure Daniel was hiding something, but whatever it was, it wasn't worth her father's health.

"I know and I am sorry." Daniel ran a hand over his glum face before taking a breath and changing the subject. "Did you find anything about the baron?"

"I did! He was walking with another gentleman. He called him Ashton, and I think he might be the brother to the Miss Ashton that Miss Belvedere mentioned. They went into a club, so I couldn't follow them, but I heard him mention he was having a ball soon. What I can't understand is that he looks like he is around thirty years old. I don't know how he could be older."

Daniel looked away, hesitating almost before he replied, "Some demons employ different ways to keep their youth, sometimes for hundreds of years."

Ember frowned, taking in what Daniel had said. She hadn't really believed that the baron could be *that* old and here

Daniel was saying it *was* possible. His mentioning of 'different ways' piqued her interest. "How does the baron do it?" she asked.

"I don't know, but if we had the book …" Daniel looked towards the kitchen.

"The Codex?" Ember frowned. "I thought it was lost."

"Apparently so," but Daniel did not look convinced.

Ember sipped her tea, trying to sound nonchalant, "I have an idea."

Daniel didn't answer, but raised his eyebrows, waiting for her to continue. "I want to go to the ball the baron is holding."

"No." Daniel's teacup clattered in the saucer as he almost dropped his cup. "Absolutely not, it's too dangerous."

"Look," countered Ember, as she had prepared for this reaction. "We haven't got any proper information on where Lady Fordingworth is, and with each day that passes she could be in more danger. All the leads so far point to the baron being involved. There may be some gossip at the ball, or other people I can ask."

"I don't like this, Ember. You're not ready yet." Daniel shook his head, worry etched on his face.

"We don't have that sort of time, Daniel." Ember looked at him, her jaw set. "Do you have any other ideas?"

"No, I don't," he sighed, not meeting her eyes.

"Then you agree?" She felt hopeful that she had won him round.

"All right, but I'm still not happy about it," Daniel conceded grimly.

"Good," said Ember firmly, ignoring the last part of what he said. She felt like she had won a small victory.

"How are you going to get your father to agree?" Daniel asked. "I am not telling him."

'Coward," Ember teased, but refused to let her father's feelings on the matter hinder her determination. "It is not his decision to make. Now," Ember straightened, eager to get the ball rolling, "how do I get an invite?"

Daniel looked thoughtful for a minute. "There might be a way. Leave it with me."

Ember was pleased. "And a dress, I will need a dress."

Chapter Eight

E mber was at the palace early the next morning. She had shown a token Daniel had given her to one of the liveried guards at a side gate and had been directed to another building on the grounds. There was a small, wood-panelled lobby adorned with ornate carvings that opened to a large main hall decked out in an array of bewildering looking equipment. Off the main hall were a couple of doors that left Ember wondering what was behind them..

"Good morning," Daniel greeted, waiting for her in the hall.

"Good morning, Daniel. This is a magnificent building," Ember enthused, looking round her with appreciation.

Daniel smiled. "This is a gymnasium, where guards and members of the royal household have trained for centuries."

Ember looked around her in awe and a sense of excitement, thinking of the history held between the walls, the kings and princes who had trained here.

"The other rooms are also for training, sparring and weapons practice." He noticed the bundle she held in her arms and said, "There are no changing rooms for women, but as it is just us using this place this morning, you can change through there." Daniel indicated a door just off the entrance. At least she hadn't travelled across town in her trousers.

The changing room had rows of low benches and a large sink in the corner. Smelling of stale sweat and maleness, she wrinkled her nose at the odour but changed quickly and joined Daniel back in the hall.

"You need to build strength and fitness first and today we will also start learning some combat skills," Daniel explained. "So first we will be doing a circuit of the equipment. Usually I would also advocate running to improve fitness. The guards run round the grounds, but I think it might be best if you are not seen by the family."

Ember frowned at this. "What does it matter if someone sees me? It is only the royal household, is it not?"

Daniel looked abashed. "Her Majesty, she, err ... does not agree with ladies taking part in too much physical exercise."

"But she has let me come here to train," Ember argued, gesturing to the hall.

"She doesn't know," said Daniel flatly.

"Oh," Ember frowned, slightly offended that the queen didn't approve of women taking exercise, she thought it was a bizarre notion. "How did you manage to arrange it then?"

"The hall is not used at this time of day and I suggested I was instructing you in matters important to the case."

"I am surprised she did not suggest we use the library," Ember countered.

Daniel coughed a laugh, "She did, and after our session here, that is where we will go so if anyone questions you, you can tell them you were there."

"Well, we have to make the most of what time we have

here. "Now," she started, pointing to a rope tied to a broad beam high above her head, "what is this for?"

After two hours, Ember stood, bent over, hands on her knees, panting. She wasn't sure which part of her was most tired—her arms, her legs, her lungs, or her mind trying to remember it all.

In addition to repeating the exercises she had learnt the previous day at home, Daniel had her climb the rope, over the beam, and back down again. She had climbed until her arms felt like jelly and then ran up and down the hall, round objects, clambering and leaping over the various structures.

At length she stood up, her sweat-soaked hair hung limply. Though most of it was still in the plait she had made that morning, some of it wisped around her face. What she really wanted was a bath, preferably a long hot soak. They didn't have one at home, so she would have to visit the public baths later.

Once she had recovered her breath and grabbed a drink of water, they moved to combat techniques.

Taking a short staff, Daniel showed her how to stand and hold it, then how to use it both defensively and for attacking. He started with some slow, easy movements at first as it felt unfamiliar, but he didn't let her go too long before he was pushing and attacking, forcing her to block and move. "Ow!" she exclaimed when she didn't block fast enough and Daniel's staff caught her arm.

Daniel's face twisted into a knowing smile. "Do you want me to go easy on a woman?"

Ember's eyes flashed as she went on the attack and soon had Daniel dancing backwards from her onslaught.

"Good," he grinned. "But control that anger, don't let it all out at once. Learn to use it and wield it. That's enough for now, we will try some other weapons."

Daniel crossed the hall and opened one of the doors, beckoning Ember to follow. She stood on the threshold and gasped. She had never seen such an array of weapons— swords of all sizes, from epees to broadswords, long staffs and pikes. Maces and other gruesome looking instruments were arranged in racks and one wall was covered in a range of bows and crossbows.

"Wow," Ember entered and turned a full circle, her eyes alight. "Is this the armoury?"

"No, the armoury is elsewhere, these are just for practice."

Ember turned towards Daniel, "What can I try? A bow and arrow?"

"Not today. I thought we should start with something smaller and more discreet"

Ember's face fell a little.

"But no less deadly," Daniel continued.

He crossed to a cabinet and drew out a wide drawer. Arranged in neat rows were knives. More types than Ember could imagine existed.

"This drawer is full of daggers, to be used for close combat." Daniel closed the drawer and opened the next one down. "These are throwing knives. Would you like to try some?"

Ember nodded and Daniel chose a few from the array in front of them. The weapons room was long and the wall at the end was lined with a thick panel of woven straw. Round targets at different heights were painted on it, along with painted shapes of people.

"That is the target wall. The targets represent different areas of the anatomy, and of course we have the outlines to help aim for certain areas," Daniel explained.

Ember could feel a wave of nausea bubble up through her. It must have shown on her face as Daniel turned back to her and said, "Are you all right? Are you tired? Do you want to rest?"

Ember shook her head slightly, but keeping her eyes on the targets, she said quietly, "It's just, I never really considered that I would be hitting live things, people."

Daniel's face softened slightly, but his voice was stern, "What did you think you were going to be aiming for? This isn't a game, Ember. This really could be a matter of life or death." He sighed, turning back to the cabinet "You asked for this, but maybe your father was right, you shouldn't be doing this." He started to put the knives away, but Ember caught his arm.

"No, I will be all right. I just need a minute."

"Honestly, Ember," Daniel started with genuine concern in his voice, "if you can't do this then stop now, because you will get hurt. You have to be one hundred percent sure you are going to be able to throw this. A second's hesitation could be fatal."

Ember swallowed, trying to push down the fear that rose with Daniel's warning. She knew hunting was dangerous, but what other choice did she have? With a nod she hoped looked confident, she replied, "Let's do this."

Daniel's smile was brief as he collected the knives again and closed the drawer. "If it helps, remember they aren't people, they are monsters—monsters who hurt and kill people." He turned to face her. "Ready?"

Ember took a deep breath, "Yes, I'm ready."

Daniel demonstrated the correct way to hold the knife in her hand and then how to draw her arm back and release it. The knife thudded into the panel, close to the centre of one of the targets.

"Your turn," he said, handing Ember one of the knives.

Ember tried to do the same as Daniel, but the knife bounced off the target and clattered onto the floor.

Ember frowned. Daniel had made it look easy.

"Don't flick your wrist," Daniel said, handing her another knife.

Ember stood looking down at the far wall. As she drew her arm up again, she had a recollection of throwing something else—*stones*, she thought. Her mother stood beside her and the words *Aim true, Firefly* came into her head. Ember let the knife go and it embedded itself into the panel right next to Daniel's, though slightly closer to the centre of the target.

Daniel narrowed his eyes at her and then looked at the target before blowing out a breath. "Whooo, not bad. Beginners luck or have you done this before?"

Ember shrugged, "Beginner's luck I guess."

He handed her two more knives. "Try again."

Those knives landed in the centre of the target, as did the following dozen knives he passed her. Soon all the targets on the wall, round and man-shaped, had knives in or close to the middle of the target.

"Impressive," said Daniel chuckling. "I guess you have found a weapon that suits you. It took me years to get even close to that score. C'mon, let's get some refreshment."

Ember saw a sink in the changing rooms so she could at least freshen up. As she put her dress back on, it suddenly felt too constrictive. She didn't have a boned bodice like some ladies wore, not having a maid to help her put it on, but even so, the many skirts and layers of fabric felt heavy and weighed her down. *I will have to do something about this*, she thought.

Ember was glad for the tea that had been served in the

library, and as soon as the servant had shut the door, she devoured half the sandwiches that accompanied it. The morning's work had left her feeling very hungry.

Daniel pushed a card across the table towards her while she ate. It was beautifully decorated and written in a very handsome script.

"Who is Miss Emmeline Duval?" she asked, reading from the card.

"You, or rather who you *will* be at the ball tomorrow night," Daniel answered.

Ember grinned delightedly, "Thank you. Duval, that's French, isn't it?"

"Yes, you are a third-generation immigrant, having fled France during the revolution. You are a distant cousin to Lady Peyton, whom you are visiting from Bath where you live. Lady Peyton will accompany you to the dance. You can speak French, I take it?"

"Oui monsieur," answered Ember, pleased her parents had been keen on making sure she knew both French and German languages. "Does Lady Peyton know who I really am?"

"Our cause has one or two patrons," Daniel explained. "Lady Peyton is one of them, so yes, she does know. You will go to her house tomorrow at three and prepare for the ball. You will travel with her to the ball, and she also has a suitable outfit for you."

"Thank you, Daniel," she replied sincerely, hoping he could tell how much the opportunity meant to her. Ember had never been to a ball before and whilst she knew it was serious business which took her there, she couldn't contain her delight in the chance of seeing the sights, the dresses, and the dancing.

"Don't forget you are there to keep a low profile," warned Daniel. "Listen for information and stay away from the baron."

"Yes, yes," Ember said, but she was still staring at the invitation card, caught up in the idea of the ball.

Suddenly she looked up and exclaimed, "Oh, but what about my father?"

"I will spend the evening with him," said Daniel, causing Ember's shoulders to sag with relief. She felt shame that she had almost forgotten him in her excitement at the prospect of the ball. She reassured herself that after she solved the case, her focus would return to supporting her father and his health.

"Thank you," replied Ember. "I think he would like that"

"As would I," agreed Daniel, leaning back a relaxed smile.

"I had better be getting back to him now," Ember said, rising from the chair.. "He was looking after the shop. Sam was looking in on him, but he is inclined to get a bit distracted. Will you visit again later? Shall we go out again tonight?"

"I think you have done enough for one day, but spend some time on your exercises. It is as important to practise those, as well as building your physical strength," Daniel replied as he rose to escort her out. "Come again tomorrow morning and we will go through it all once more before the ball."

Ember left the palace and started towards home. *I do need better clothes,* she thought, noticing that Sam's trousers weren't really a good fit, especially round her hips. She needed something loose fitting.

As she drew closer to the shop, she reflected on her training. Although she was very weary, it had made her feel alive and she wanted more of it, much more. Today's practice has sparked something inside of her, and she wasn't afraid to put in the work if it meant she'd be prepared for whatever came her way.

Chapter Nine

After the busyness of the last few days, Ember was glad of an evening of peace and quiet. While she led an active life, she didn't do any physical training and she was tired after her training that morning, her shoulders ached and her legs felt heavy. She was never going to admit that to Daniel though. She was a little ashamed she had shown some weakness when confronted with the realisation that she might have to use these skills on living things.

She still wasn't reconciled to the idea, but she wasn't going to let herself slip again. It was clear she couldn't afford to let Daniel believe she wasn't capable and strong enough for this. Stretching from her chair by the fire, she rose and went through to the shop, running her fingers along the spines until she found the tome she was looking for.

A Treatise on Calisthenic Exercises for Women—Signor Voarino's book. She had known about the book, they had a couple of other similar titles in the shop, but hadn't really taken them seriously. She leafed through the pages seeing if there was anything that would help. There were some interesting exercises. Some included using a cane, lifting it up and behind the head to stretch the shoulders while performing lunges with each leg in turn. Others involved standing on one leg, then bending and straightening it again, which required excellent balance as she found out when first trying them. Ember thought she could do some of these daily to improve her fitness level. She tried a couple of the stretches and the aches from yesterday's training eased a little. She remembered how she felt when they encountered the woodwolf and was determined to do all she could to never feel that helpless again.

As she returned Voarino's book to the shelf, the hunter's journals that Daniel had brought over a few days previously caught her eye. Sitting down at the table, she pulled one towards her, reflecting on how much had occurred in such a short space of time.

Notes on the Origins of Dreachen.

She soon became absorbed in the book, losing track of time, fascinated at the very different world it described compared to what she thought she knew. It was so like the fairy stories and tales by the Grimm brothers she had read, but the thought of them being real gave an extra thrill, along with a despondency that there was so much she didn't yet know. She learned how there have been times when the veils between worlds were thin, and doorways to other realms had been opened, allowing through the passage of non-human creatures. Shapeshifters and demons mostly.

This had been going on for centuries and according to the book, most continents had several of these portals. Some of the portals had been closed or destroyed, but there were many still active.

It put forward a theory that witches had been created when demons and humans had mated, the changes over generations leading to some specific traits which were enhanced through spells and totems.

She looked to see if there was anything about the hunters, but drew a blank. There wasn't much information on the different types of demons in the books either, at least nothing like the creature she had seen a couple of nights ago. This was frustrating as she wanted more answers on what she could do.

Ember sat musing about what she knew so far. If she hadn't seen demons with her own eyes, she would never have believed in them. But now she could feel a sensation building in her, almost like she needed to seek them out.

Where was the Codex? She was pretty sure she hadn't seen something that old in the shop, but it wouldn't hurt to have another look. She decided to start at the top and work her way down as the first floor was usually where the older and rarer books were kept.

She ascended the iron spiral staircase and walked between the shelves, paying particular attention to anything that looked unfamiliar to her or was bound in the same fashion as the journals Daniel had brought. She recalled how she used to love finding books her mother and father sent her to seek, always being able to discover them eventually. She felt frustrated that this one alluded her.

After scouting out all of the upper floor, she leaned on the railings at the top of the stairs and looked down over the main part of the bookshop. Whilst most shelves were floor to ceiling, in this section, where the bookshop was double height, the shelves were shorter and she could see the tops of some of them. A couple of the shelves had books piled on top and she started to admonish herself for being untidy and not putting them away correctly when she noticed a stack she hadn't seen before. A thrill ran through her—*was one of these the Codex?*

She ran down the stairs and reached for the wooden step

ladders used to access the upper shelves. She pulled down the small stack of books, hardly able to breathe in anticipation. She placed them on the study table and read the titles. Disappointment flooded through her as she realised it was *Sir Walter Scott's Letters on Demonology and Witchcraft*. A book of folklore and superstition, and whilst interesting, it was widely published—hardly the Codex Daniel had referred to. She sat down at the table with a sigh. If it wasn't in the shop, then that left the rest of the house. It must be somewhere. She believed Daniel when he said it couldn't be lost. She knew there was nowhere to hide a book in the parlour and kitchen, but she had a quick scan anyway. She hoped it wasn't in the cellar as it had a tendency to be damp. Taking a candle, she made her way down the steps, smiling to herself at how she used to run down here. It was one of her favourite hideaways for hide and seek. There wasn't much in the cellar nowadays, just some dwindling coal supplies and a few packing crates that books arrived in. She checked these, but they were all empty.

That left her bedroom, and she knew it wasn't in there. *What about Father's bedroom?* Surely he would know if the book was in his room and he was adamant that he didn't know of its whereabouts. That left only the attics.

Ember hadn't been in the attic rooms for many years. She cracked open the door and looked at the dusty cobwebs that crisscrossed the room. Despite the late hour, she collected a duster and started to clear the cobwebs away. The attics were mostly for storage, old toys she had long grown out of and some trunks. She spied one she recognised—it had belonged to her mother. Sitting down in front of it, she tentatively opened the lid. Laid at the top was her mother's vanity set—a beautiful silver-backed brush, comb, and mirror. She knew that no matter how poor they were, her father would never pawn them. Her mother's scent wafted up and a cry caught in

Ember's throat as she remembered being enveloped in her mother's arms where hugs were freely given. Ember looked further into the trunk. There were several of her mother's favourite dresses folded neatly. Ember gathered them to herself, burying her face in them. She wished more than anything that she had her mother to talk to right now.

Chapter Ten

When Ember arrived at the gymnasium the following morning, Daniel's eyebrows rose at her attire but he nodded his approval. Ember had remembered seeing people in the Chinese quarter wearing a tunic and loose trousers. After training the previous day, she had taken a couple of tomes they had in Chinese to the docks at Limehouse—the Chinese area of the city— and managed to swap them for a navy blue suit and some soft shoes. The cloth was lightweight and very freeing. She joined the training session with enthusiasm and felt the loose clothing definitely helped.

"How do you feel?" Daniel asked her before they started.

"Fine," Ember replied breezily, though in truth she did ache a little from the previous day's training.

"It is always the second day that it really hurts." Ember shot him a dark look, but Daniel merely grinned in response. She wasn't going to let him think she was weak.

The training was a repeat of the previous day—circuit training, some work with a short staff, followed by weapons practice. If anything, Ember's aim with the knives was even better.

"How do you do that?" asked Daniel with an amused smile. "You must have a really good eye for aiming."

"I don't know," Ember answered honestly. She was just as perplexed about her unusual talent as Daniel. "I don't really think about it, other than where I want the knife to go."

"Well, it's extraordinary," replied Daniel, visibly impressed. "Now we will do a short session with daggers, but it really does require skill and practice to wield effectively."

Ember watched warily as Daniel donned a bulky, straw suit and swallowed her unease when she realised she'd be working with a live target. He showed Ember the places to aim for with the dagger. "Here," he said, indicating a place adjacent to his lower ribs. Ember tentatively poked the dagger at him, terrified of hurting him.

"No, harder," Daniel ordered.

Ember tried again with more force and the knife went in a little way.

"Even harder," Daniel cried again.

This time Ember thrust with force and the dagger went straight in, up to the hilt.

"That's better. Remember there are no second chances when faced with a monster."

Ember reeled a little from the amount of force she had to use. She wasn't sure she would be able to do it for real if she found it this difficult in training."It is harder than I thought it would be!"

"It is," Daniel conceded, which Ember was momentarily grateful for. "But some dreachen have a tough hide rather than soft skin. Now again." Ember gritted her teeth, determined that she could do it as Daniel made her go through several more attempts before he was happy she had gotten the basics down.

Daniel eventually called a halt to the training. Ember was glad of the rest and fetched them both a glass of water. She noticed Daniel looking pensive.

"What is it?" she asked, wondering if she had done something wrong.

He sighed, his face serious. "I really don't like sending you out into the field, as we call it, without a lot more training. But we are out of time, so this will have to do and"—Daniel paused, making sure he had her attention—"if you stay out of trouble, you won't need to use these techniques at all."

"I know, I will only try to find out information on where Lady Margaret might be held," said Ember.

"Yes, then we will work out a plan *together* to get her out."

❖

After Ember had changed back into her dress, they headed to the bookshop. Ember enjoyed the spring air, which was more sun than smog for once. As they walked, Daniel drilled her on what to do at the ball, to stay close to Lady Peyton, and to not wander off on her own. Once she had promised to do exactly as he advised he changed the subject.

"How is Mr Hinton's invention coming along?"

"Sam?" Ember asked, brought out of her reverie of trying to imagine what the ball would be like. She could hardly contain her excitement to finally be attending one and pushed the reasons why to the back of her mind. "The last time I saw it, I got covered in black soot, but I'm sure he will have sorted it by now."

"Do you think he would let me have a look sometime?" Daniel asked.

Ember laughed as they reached the bookshop. "I am sure he would be more than happy to have another person to show off to."

There had been a few book sales recently so lunch consisted of bread with both cheese and cold meats. Ember was grateful Daniel didn't get to see that all they had some days was bread dipped in thinned gravy from the previous day's supper. Ember was hoping that if she could find the heiress soon, she would have enough money to make a real supper before taking her father away from the smog of the city.

After lunch Ember took the plates from her father and Daniel into the scullery to wash up while Daniel brewed a pot of tea. Accepting a cup from him, she settled into a chair for a few moments' rest before she needed to leave to prepare for the ball.

"How did you two meet?" Ember aimed the question at both of them.

Daniel looked over at Robert and he waved his hand, apparently giving Daniel permission to tell the story. He nodded and turned back to Ember.

"We were both young, probably about your age. I had just arrived in London. I grew up in York," he explained. Ember was surprised— she had assumed he had been born in London, like her father.

"I had been on the trail of a dreachen who had fled York, but I didn't know my way around London very well. I was tracking the demon and ended up in a dead-end alley and no way out. What I didn't know was your father had also picked up the trail of the demon. I turned round to leave the alley and bumped straight into him."

Robert snorted and Ember and Daniel both looked at him. Ember could see amusement in his eyes trying to hide a smirk.

Daniel smiled as he continued, "We both went flying, and ended up on the floor. Your father might be laughing now," he glanced again at Robert with a grin before turning back to Ember. "But he wasn't back then. I remember he had quite a lot to say about clumsy country boys. Not that I was a country boy, York *is* a city.

"Once he had calmed down, I let his tirade run its course. I pointed out that we could stand there all night and argue or we could track the demon together. He required little convincing because back then, as there is now, there was a lack of hunters on the streets of London."

"Did you catch the demon?" Ember asked, intrigued.

Robert replied this time. "We did run it to the ground a couple of days later and I am glad we were able to work together as it was particularly tricky. It was no surprise it had evaded capture for so long. We decided then to team up and work together," her father explained, grinning at Daniel.

It was clear they wanted to reminisce some more so, leaving her father and Daniel talking, Ember took a few minutes to pop over the street and see Sam.

"Hi, Sammy," she called, causing Sam to straighten up from bending over the machine in the middle of his workshop.

"Hi, Em." He wiped his hands on a rag and picked up a parcel from a bench. As he handed her the small package he asked, "What are you getting yourself into?"

"It's just an investigation job, Sam," she tried to sound dismissive, hoping he wouldn't pry any further.

"Is your gentleman still there?"

Ember scoffed. "Sam, you know he is not my *gentleman*—he is an old friend of my pa's."

"He seems to be around an awful lot," sniffed Sam, and Ember was surprised he had noticed.

"He is good company for Pa and they used to work

together, so he has been helping me make a few new contacts. If I am going to make a success out of the business on my own, I will need more of those. I might even find you a wealthy backer."

She gave Sam a friendly nudge. "How's it going anyway?"

Sam looked pleased she had asked. "I hope to have the adjustments finished later. Would you like to see?"

Ember shook her head slightly, feeling guilty that she hadn't been around much lately. She sighed, knowing that it wasn't going to get better just yet, but it would be worth it once she found Lady Fordingworth. "Sorry, Sam. I have to go out tonight, but I will come round tomorrow and I may bring my gentleman," she teased. "Thanks again," she said, gesturing to the package, and gave him a quick squeeze before she left.

"I don't want you to do this." Robert was leaning on the door frame in the kitchen watching Ember pull on her hat and coat.

"Oh Papa, I know. But we need to eat, to keep this place." Ember regretted the words as soon as she saw the look of hurt that crossed her father's face. She knew he felt bad that he couldn't work, but the reality was she needed to earn money. She crossed the room and took his hands in her own.

"I promise I will be careful. It is just a missing person case and when I find the heiress, we can go away for a bit, get some sea air."

Robert took a deep breath, tears glistening in his eyes. "You are just like her, you know. She would have been very proud of you." Ember couldn't speak, a lump had formed in her throat. She squeezed her father's hands and gave him a sad smile.

"Are you ready?" Daniel called from the door. "Lady Peyton's carriage is here."

"Just be careful," Robert said quietly before releasing her hands. "I couldn't bear to lose you too."

Chapter Eleven

It wasn't a long drive to Lady Peyton's house and after approximately thirty minutes, Ember felt the carriage turn into a driveway. Stepping down, Ember looked round her. It wasn't just the large square Georgian house that caught her attention, but the noise, or rather its absence. Ember had lived all her life in London, she was used to the sounds, the clamour at all hours, but here, even though they were just south of the river near Kew gardens, it was quiet. The grounds were surrounded by a high wall and bordered with tall trees and bushes, which blocked out the noise and made Ember feel like she was in a different world. She hadn't realised she had turned round with her eyes wide until she heard a voice behind her.

"A little oasis of calm isn't it?"

Ember spun round to the source of the voice and saw a lady, who Ember presumed to be around sixty, standing at the top of the steps in the open doorway. She was quite tall, and had a very upright bearing. Her clothes were very fine in an understated and elegant way. At length, Ember realised she was probably Lady Peyton.

"Oh, sorry," she dropped her eyes and bobbed a curtsey.

The lady smiled. "Come child, we have much to do and not much time." She beckoned Ember towards her and turned without waiting to see if Ember followed her. As soon as she was through the door she called out, "Dotty, please ready a bath for Miss Merrington."

"Um, Lady Peyton?" Ember enquired.

"Good, I see you are not completely devoid of intelligence," Lady Peyton replied imperiously.

Ember swallowed, "I ..."

"Don't worry, just my little joke, and you must call me Aunt Louisa."

Ember was taken aback. She hadn't known the lady for more than a few minutes.

Seeing Ember's concern, she continued, "Aunt Louisa, for tonight you must call me Aunt Louisa."

"Ah yes," Ember said, relieved. "Of course, Aunt Louisa."

Lady Peyton softened slightly. "In ideal circumstances, we would have weeks to prepare for this, but we have just a few hours. Now follow Dotty, she is pouring you a bath. Once you are done, join me in the dining room and we will do what we can while we take afternoon tea."

"Thank you, La—Aunt Louisa," said Ember before following the maid who was carrying a jug up the stairs. With each step, she couldn't help but feel the night was going to be an adventure, one she hoped she was ready for.

❖

Ember sat in the bath and looked out the window. She had only ever used the public bath houses, so she never had the chance to look out the window while she washed, or not have to be aware of the women standing outside her cubicle urging her to hurry up. The water was deliciously warm and smelt wonderful. She didn't know what the maid had tipped into the bath, but it smelt like a flower meadow on a summer's day. Ember could have spent all afternoon luxuriating in the warm scented water, but eventually the water started to go cold and she was aware she needed to spend time preparing with Lady Peyton.

She stepped out of the bath and was towelling herself dry with a plump soft towel—a far cry from the threadbare ones that she had at home—when the maid knocked and entered. She was carrying a robe which she handed to Ember.

"Please, miss, Madam is waiting in the dining room for you. When you are ready, head down the stairs and it's the left-hand door."

Ember thanked her as she accepted the robe. It was soft and shimmered slightly, the fabric rich blue and embroidered with peacocks in vibrant colours of red, green and gold. *Is this silk?* thought Ember, not that she had ever felt it before. She realised she was in unfamiliar territory, a world she had never seen before, and she knew she wasn't equal to it, but she would do her best.

Wrapping the robe round herself and tying it closed with the belt, she picked up the towel and rubbed her hair with it while she descended the stairs.

❖

"Ah, come in child, sit by the fire and dry your hair. How was your bath?" Lady Peyton gestured to the fire where a low stool was placed.

"It was lovely, thank you." Ember sat and looked round the

room. The walls were covered in wallpaper with a vine pattern. Heavy drapes hung at the windows, And there was a large mahogany table in the centre of the room surrounded by eight matching chairs.

Lady Peyton sat on one side of the fire and there was another chair pushed back against the wall. The coverings and cushions were decorated with brightly coloured embroidery depicting all manner of birds. Large pictures hung on the walls featuring scenes of people and animals.

"They are places I have visited, some are of where I have lived," explained Lady Peyton, and Ember realised that she must have been staring at the paintings. She turned her attention back to Lady Peyton and continued drying her hair, combing her hands through the strands, letting the heat of the fire dry it.

"Are they of India?" asked Ember. She had spent many hours poring over books showing different parts of the world —places she longed to visit, not that she would get the chance. Names like Africa and India sounded exotic to her and she recognised the animals from the books.

"Yes, I have lived there most of my life," Lady Peyton replied. "We don't have enough time to give you a full history, but I will tell you enough to give you a background for tonight. I was born in England and grew up here. I met my husband during my first London season and then when I was about your age, he was sent to India, as assistant to a commander. He worked his way up the ranks and within a few years was given his own posting overseeing an outpost." Lady Peyton paused and looked into the fire for a moment before taking a deep breath.

"Sadly, he was killed ten years ago. I stayed on in India for a while as I had some projects I was invested in, schools and hospitals, but five years ago, after thirty-five years in the colonies, I decided it was time to return back to the land of my birth. I bought Lyndon Lodge then and I have tried to keep up with London society, but a lot has changed while I was away. Sometimes I wish I had stayed there." She looked a little sad and Ember didn't know what to say. Then Lady Peyton brightened up.

"But tonight we are going to have some fun, aren't we?"

Ember wasn't sure about that. Lady Peyton's story had diverted her for a few moments, but she couldn't ignore that she felt fidgety and was trying to slow her breathing down by taking deeper breaths. "I hope so."

"You will need nerves of steel. Ah, now eat some food, that will help with the nerves." The door had opened and the maid who filled her bath entered, while a younger maid followed with a tray of tea things, some sandwiches and small cakes.

"There will be food at the ball tonight, but we need something to keep us going until then," Lady Peyton explained. "Now help yourself, dear." She waved her hand towards the table. Ember found that she was rather hungry, so she selected a few sandwiches from the tray.

"Can I pour you some tea, Aunt Louisa?" asked Ember, the name and title unfamiliar to her. She had never had a female relative apart from her mother, and she realised with a stab of sadness that she knew nothing about her mother's family at all.

"Yes please, dear," replied Lady Peyton with a smile. "There, look how well we are doing already."

Ember put the cup and saucer on a small table next to her chair and held out the plate of sandwiches. Lady Peyton selected a few and Ember returned to her seat by the fire to take a bite of her own. They were delicious and she noticed that she had devoured several within the space of a few minutes.

"Yes, you do need feeding up a little." Lady Peyton looked at her empty plate approvingly, "Please help yourself, they won't eat themselves."

When Ember returned to her seat after filling her plate again, Lady Peyton continued. "Now back to work. you will be Emmeline Duval, I chose that name myself." The woman's eyes twinkled. "Your family originated from France and fled during the Revolution, and your great grandmother married one of my late husband's cousins. That should be distant enough for those who care for such matters to not wonder why you have never been mentioned before."

Ember ate her sandwiches and nodded. "You grew up in Bath and your mother wants you to learn something of London society, but she cannot accompany you as she is unwell and it just so happens I want a companion for the summer." Lady Peyton paused. "With me so far?"

Ember nodded again, "Yes, Aunt Louisa."

"The arrangements were all rather last minute and you arrived yesterday. I did not want to change my arrangements and miss the dance, which is why I requested an invite for you." Lady Peyton beamed. "See, it has all worked out rather well. Now tell all that back to me so I know you have got it."

Ember did so and Lady Peyton exclaimed, "I haven't had so much fun in years."

Ember released a breath and smiled, happy that Lady Peyton was pleased with her. Despite her nerves and worries about the night ahead, she liked Lady Peyton and was glad she had her with her tonight. "Can I ask a question?" Ember said hesitantly.

"Yes, of course, child, though I might choose not to answer it," laughed Lady Peyton.

Ember frowned a little. She had never met such a lively and forward character as Lady Peyton. Her straight manner took some getting used to, but Ember did like her a lot. She decided to ask anyway.

"How do you know Mr Beresford?"

"Ah, young Daniel, I have known him for a good twenty years or more. He used to come out to the colonies and helped my husband with a few troubles we were having, on more than one occasion." *Demons?* wondered Ember.

"Though I was a dab hand with a sword myself in my younger years."

Ember's eyes widened as Lady Peyton continued, "Oh yes, why should the men have all the fun?"

Ember decided she liked Lady Peyton even more. "Though we could have done with his help the last time," Lady Peyton paused, her voice sounding mournful. "Maybe my Edgar would still be alive." She sighed heavily. "Ah well, what is done is done and here we are now."

Ember knew what it was like to lose someone dear to them and hated that someone as vivacious as Lady Peyton had suffered such a tragic loss. She crossed to the old lady and, placing her arms around her while she sat, gave her a hug. Lady Peyton was staring into the fire but she clasped Ember's arm with her hand and whispered, "Thank you, my dear."

Ember released her and poured them both another cup of tea as tea was always her go to comfort. Lady Peyton smiled at Ember as she took the cup, her eyes still glistening with tears.

After a few minutes, she put down her cup and took a deep breath. "Now this won't do. Let us be melancholy another time, for tonight we will have some fun. Pop into the hall and call for Dotty please, my dear."

❖

Ember turned in front of the mirror, marvelling at her

own reflection. She hardly recognised the woman looking back at her. The young maid, Kitty, had piled her hair on her head, managing to tame some of her wispy strands into ringlets. The whole arrangement was held together with an ornate comb at the back of her head.

The dress Lady Peyton had chosen for her was exquisite. Ember rubbed the material between her fingers, wondering what it was.

"Tis taffeta, miss," Kitty said as she helped Ember into the dress. The bodice was fitted perfectly, leading to a full skirt that swayed deliciously as she moved from side to side. There was a chiffon overshirt with short chiffon sleeves that fell off her shoulders. The whole dress was blue, graduating from very pale at the top, which was adorned with blue gems, to a deep blue at bottom, where tiny pearls looked like stars in the night sky.

There were some blue satin dancing slippers to complete the look. She hoped she wouldn't be doing much more than dancing in them as they looked rather flimsy.

Kitty smiled at her. "You look lovely, miss."

"Thank you, you have done wonders with my hair. I can never do anything like that myself, so I usually give up and just braid it." Kitty beamed at her and left.

Ember spied her clothes and coat on the bed and remembered the package she had bought with her. Carefully unwrapping it, she ran her fingers over the leather tooled surface. Sam had done a good job, even with the small amount of time he had, it was a thing of beauty. She gently lifted her dress and buckled it to her thigh. Reaching into her coat, she pulled out a short dagger she had taken from her father's black chest and slid it into the holder Sam had made, along with a set of lock picks. As she settled her skirt, she checked that they couldn't be seen and smiled at the mirror. Now she felt ready. She hoped she wouldn't have to use them, but she couldn't help but feel a little less nervous knowing they were there.

Reaching for the dark blue velvet cloak Lady Peyton had supplied, she gave her reflection a final nod, prepared for whatever the evening might hold.

Chapter Twelve

As Ember stood at the top of the stairs to the ballroom from the entrance lobby, she felt a wave of panic wash over her. *What was I thinking of? How did I ever think I could pull this off?* She tried to fight the urge to turn and run. Lady Peyton must have felt her tense up as she reached for her hand and pulled it through her arm. "Relax, child," she whispered, "we are all playing a part here. You will be fine."

She then started to tell Ember who people were and little snippets of gossip, which soon had Ember smiling despite her nerves. "Oh, look at Mrs Pomfrey. Doesn't that hat look ghastly? And her daughter must be the oldest spinster in the room."

Ember suppressed a laugh as she continued to gaze around her. She had never seen a ballroom before. It was a huge room, high ceilinged with crystal chandeliers powered by the latest in gaslight technology. One side of the room had glass doors, open to the stone terrace, that almost reached to the ceiling and were framed by green and gold curtains.The walls were white with panels of painted scenes edged with gilded cornices and fascias. Golden benches adorned with green velvet cushions were placed along the walls for weary dancers and those who wanted to watch the dancing. On the wall opposite the windows were a series of archways leading to small rooms where tables were arranged to give space for groups to gather and chat, and in a few, card games were in progress. A quartet of musicians were staged at one end and Ember was already feeling the effects of the music. Despite her mission, she really wanted to dance.

Better than the room and its decorations were the people themselves. Ember marvelled at the dresses in all colours and fashions worn by the most elegant of ladies. Tiaras, head-dresses of feathers, and exotic turbans sat atop the latest hair-styles. In front of the mirror at Lyndon Lodge Ember had almost felt overdressed, but here she felt she was just a daisy in a bed of roses.

"I think we need a drink," Lady Peyton said and steered them over to a table set with a large punchbowl and an array of crystal glasses. Ember poured a glass and as she was handing one to Lady Peyton, another lady of a similar age appeared. She was accompanied by a young lady roughly Ember's age.

"Ah," Lady Peyton said. "Let me introduce my cousin's daughter, Emmeline Duval, to you." Turning to Ember, she said, "Lady Harcourt and her granddaughter, Miss Felicia Worthing." Ember bobbed a quick curtsey and Lady Harcourt inclined her head slightly. "Duval? Are you French?"

Ember smiled, trying to not let her nerves show, and remembered Lady Peyton's words that they were all playing a part. "Qui, madam, but my family have been in England for a long time."

Before Lady Harcourt could respond, Miss Worthing spoke, "Gramama, I am going to talk to Miss Lucas." She was wearing a pink gown, layered with tiers of ruffles. Ember thought she looked a bit like the birthday cakes she had seen in the window of Fortnums and Masons.

"Of course, my dear." Lady Harcourt dismissed her and turned to Lady Peyton, launching into a lengthy tale. Ember put down her glass and Lady Peyton nodded to her, telling Ember with her eyes that she would be fine on her own for a while.

"I will see you later, Aunt Louisa, Lady Harcourt." Ember bobbed another curtsey before starting to take a stroll round the room. She watched the dancing, thinking how lovely it would be to join in. She longed to dance, but she didn't know anyone and didn't have the benefit of a friend to introduce her.

She was trying not to stare about her, but she hadn't yet seen any sign of the baron or Ashton. She took a couple of turns around the ballroom before sitting on one of the benches for a rest. As she glanced around, she noticed that there were few other young ladies sitting alone. Not wanting to draw attention to herself, she rose and took another turn. She began to worry that the baron would never arrive, and coming to the resolution that she might as well head back to Lady Peyton, she headed back towards where the woman was seated. A sudden movement caught her eyes and she saw the baron heading down the stairs. She withdrew a little into the shadows, but kept her eyes on him, watching closely as he spoke to several people. He seemed an affable and courteous host.

She stood for a few minutes, watching him in her peripheral vision and then let herself focus, seeing if she could sense that he was dreachen. She took a few calm breaths and cast out her senses. Reaching out, she felt a faint tingle. Intrigued, she pushed a little further. She allowed herself a small smile, pleased that her senses worked in this busy environment.

Then she reeled. A shockwave slammed into her mind and she let out a gasp, involuntarily taking a step backwards. She saw the baron snap his head her way. Luckily she wasn't looking directly at him and was half hidden behind a group of people in conversation. Cursing herself, she withdrew the tendrils of her focus and stepped back further, behind the group and out of his direct line of sight. *How could I be so foolish?* She stood there for a while, her heart hammering against her ribcage, shaking from the shock of nearly being caught and the realisation that she had so much yet to learn. After a few minutes, she risked a look and saw that the baron had gone. She sought out Lady Peyton and sat with her for a little while, calming her thoughts and nerves.

She recovered quickly as she didn't think she could sit through another conversation about the scandal of Mrs Tench, or whatever her name was, only serving three types of cake at her last gathering, or how it was a shame that Miss Compton was unmarried at twenty-seven. With a warm affinity for Miss Compton that she was not someone's property, Ember remembered she had come to do a job, and sitting scared in hiding wasn't going to find out more about the baron and whether he was keeping the heiress. She rested her hand on the dagger beneath her dress and felt a little more confident.

Deciding to have another look around, she stood and looked across the room. She saw the baron talking with Ashton, and beside him stood a very beautiful lady. *That must be Ashton's sister*, Ember thought. The lady certainly had her eyes on the baron and was saying something gaily to him. His lips did curl slightly but his eyes were like flint. Ashton's sister was dressed in a dark red silk gown that fit her curves perfectly. She was stunning with her blonde hair gathered on her head and secured with a glistening crystal and ruby headdress.

The baron stiffened suddenly and twisted his head slightly, as if he was listening to something, before relaxing somewhat and offering his hand to Ashton's sister for a dance. As they swept past her, Ember wanted to see if she could sense something in Ashton's sister, but dared not while she was so close to the baron.

Once they were further round the dance floor, Ember slipped out of the room. There were a few ball goers walking the corridors and Ember soon found a few other rooms where people were sitting and talking outside of the noise of the dance floor, and another where food was being served. She was grateful she had eaten something at Lyndon Lodge as she was too keyed up to be able to eat anything right now. She wandered past the dining room and found another corridor that was not lit quite so brightly. As she followed it, she realised it went towards the back of the building, and at the end were stairs heading downwards. Ember cast a quick look over her shoulder. Seeing no one, she started to descend them and found a floor below and a corridor heading off from it. The stairs continued down, and curiosity got the better of her. She started down again, then she heard a door closing from the corridor and a supercilious voice, "Can I help you?"

She whirled round and saw a liveried servant coming towards her. She was down two steps, so it felt like he towered over her. "I, err, I got lost. I was looking for the um, convenience." Ember jigged a little to show she was desperate.

That did the trick—the servant took a step back and looked at her disdainfully. "This way, miss," he said, gesturing back up the stairs. "Let me show you." He said the last part quite firmly, making sure she understood that guests were not allowed to go roaming round the house.

Ember went back up the stairs in front of the servant and when he had shown her the room, she turned and thanked him. He waited until she had gone inside.

Closing the door behind her, she leant on it for a moment. After a couple of glasses of punch, she might as well make use of the facilities while she was there. Afterwards she checked her reflection in the mirror and said to herself in an impression of Lady Peyton, "Nerves of steel, girl."

Heading back towards the dance floor she saw Miss Ashton walking towards her. Ember drew herself up a little straighter, though Miss Ashton was a couple of inches taller than she was. As they passed, Miss Ashton narrowed her eyes at Ember but then swept past her and continued down the corridor. Ember shrugged, refusing to let the pettiness of society get to her, and entered the ballroom. After checking on Lady Peyton, she took another turn round the room, disappointed that she had not been able to find out much so far.

"Mademoiselle Duval, viens danser avec moi s'il te plaît?" The voice was deep and smooth, the French spoken perfectly. Ember felt a chill down her spine and spun round to find herself face to face with the baron. She gulped, taking in his outstretched hand asking her to dance. How did he know her name? And why was he asking her? Maybe she hadn't escaped his notice earlier. Annoyance with herself at her mistake rose up, threatening to engulf her in panic. She tried to calm herself and think rationally—maybe he was just being polite as she was new and he was a gracious host. She noticed people were watching them with interest. It would be very rude to refuse the host, so she forced her mouth into a smile, and taking his hand replied, "Ce serait un plaisir."

The baron's eyes glittered in mirth as he spun her onto the dance floor. She felt ever grateful to the times she had made Sam dance with her, dreaming one day for a moment like this, though she would have preferred her first time on the dance floor to be with any other partner. She regarded him, never having seen him this close before. He had a timeless face that would be hard to pin an age to, somewhere between twenty-five and forty years old. *He was very handsome, though a bit too smooth and sure of himself,* thought Ember. His black hair, showing not a strand of grey, was slicked back from a high forehead with angular cheekbones and a chiselled chin. His grey eyes were regarding her back before his expressive mouth twisted into a little smile.

As Ember turned in the baron's arms, she saw Miss Ashton staring at her. She was standing next to Miss Worthing and turned slightly as if to ask her something before staring at Ember again, her eyes glistening like dark pebbles.

"You are wondering how I know who you are." The baron's voice was oiled with a hint of a European accent.

"No, I …" He smirked and Ember realised now that he had now spoken in English, she had answered without thinking. "I was thinking nothing of the sort," she bit back, angry with herself.

"Oh I know you can speak English very well." He spun her round in time with the music, proving that he was an excellent dancer. He pulled her close, one hand on the small of her back, and whispered into her ear, "And I know who you really are."

Ember frowned a little, trying to calm herself. Already feeling on the back foot, she wondered what exactly he knew. She decided attack was the best policy. "Then why did you allow me an invitation?" she asked.

"Because I wanted to meet you, Miss Merrington," he said with a satisfied smile. Her chest constricted and the lack of breath caused her to stumble a couple of steps. The baron expertly recovered her without breaking stride, his smile turning into a smirk. It felt strange to hear her name trip off his tongue and she felt a sense of dread that her disguise had been so transparent. This was exactly the situation Daniel had told her to avoid. She needed to find a way to escape.

"Have you come to ask about the Stroga?" he purred. Ember stiffened slightly, another word from her memory. This time she had a sudden moment of clarity—it was her mother who had taught her these words. They weren't of any languages she had heard since, and she sifted through her mind trying to find it. *Ah, Stroga meant witch.*

"I don't know what you are talking about," Ember said through gritted teeth, clinging to some belief that she could regain her composure. "I am here with my Aunt Louisa."

The baron chuckled softly. "You are very like her, you know. Your mother, Rosamund."

Ember's heart skipped a beat. *What did he know of Mother?* Rose—her mother's name was Rose—but he had said Rosamund with a heavy German accent.

"Do you not know of your mother's fame?" The baron must have felt her falter. "She was the greatest hunter of them all. She never did quite catch up with me, though it was not through lack of trying."

Ember's world went into slow motion, and her core felt chilled. What was he saying? That her mother was a *hunter*? It couldn't be true. Surely with the revelations of the last few days her father would have said something.

"My mother was a bookseller." But Ember hesitated—she didn't really know much about what her mother had done before she had been born, it was never spoken of. But then again, she did teach Ember a strange language and how to pick locks. A few other memories rose up that Ember thought were part of a normal childhood, but was suddenly not so sure.

"She was a worthy opponent with skills no mere hunter should have." The baron's smile now turned to scorn. "But all they can send now is a young girl with no training on how to sense without revealing herself. Oh yes, I felt you girl. No training at all." So she hadn't gotten away with it then. *How am I going to get out of this now?* She struggled to remove herself from his hold but he held her tighter. "I actually feel quite insulted, but I am sure the feeling will pass soon enough."

Ember now realised that as they danced, they had been moving towards one end of the room. She hadn't been paying enough attention. Just behind her were some heavy curtains across a doorway and the baron pushed her through them. "Let me go!" She started to struggle.

"Not a chance," he replied, "I can't have you meddling in my affairs."

The last thing she felt was a cloth forced over her mouth and nose and a sickly sweet scent, then the world went black.

Chapter Thirteen

E mber blinked in the gloom, waiting for her eyes to adjust to the small amount of light available. She was lying on the floor and shifted slightly to get more comfortable.

"Are you another poor witch for the baron's collection?" A voice in the dark. The sound came from behind her, so Ember slowly pushed herself up to sitting position, relieved that nothing felt broken or even sore. She turned where the sound had come from.

"I am not a witch," she replied

"Neither am I, but that doesn't stop him trying to make me be one." The voice was soft and low, albeit a bit hoarse and gravelly, but Ember could tell it was normally rich and warm.

Ember looked around in the murky light and could see that she was in a stone room. There were no windows, though a heavy wooden door was set in one wall. There was a small gap in the door with bars across it, and what little light there was came through from the corridor outside where a couple of candles burned. Straw covered an earthen floor, and there were some blankets in a corner. Another corner held a bucket, along with a foul smell. Ember coughed at the stench.

"Not pleasant, is it?" the voice spoke again. "I have had to live with my own smell for several days now. Well, I think it has been several days. It is hard to tell."

Across from Ember sat a young woman, dressed in what would have been a fine ball gown of deepest navy satin, but was now torn and dirty. Her hair, the black and blue of a raven's wing, was hanging down her face, which was lovely although smeared with dirt.

"Lady Margaret Bertilda Fordingworth?" enquired Ember.

"I see someone hasn't forgotten me. I rather thought they had."

"I have been looking for you." Ember was pleased she had at least stumbled upon her Lady La-di-da, even if the circumstances were less than ideal.

"And now you have found me, but if you are my rescue party, it's not going well, is it?" she said bluntly.

Ember ran her hand down her face and sighed. "Hmmm, I admit it could have gone better," she agreed. "On the plus side, I have found you, which was part of my job, but on the other hand, if I am going to get paid, we need to find a way to get out of here."

The voice laughed. "I like you. Please call me Tilda."

"Pleased to meet you, Tilda. I am Ember." Ember was expecting a highly strung and haughty young lady, but she liked the blunt, witty and irrepressible Tilda much better. "Tell me, why does he think you are a witch?" she asked, trying to understand what the baron would want with Tilda.

"I don't know," Tilda sighed, frustration creeping into her voice. "He says it is in my heritage, that it passes down the female line, but as far as I know my mother isn't a witch. I am sure I would have noticed. Though I have heard some odd tales of my great grandmama. Of course I had always dismissed them as tales to frighten Freddie and me when we were children."

"Freddie?" Ember queried. "A brother?"

"My twin brother, though he is up at Oxford at the moment. I am left here and very jealous of him having all the fun at college." Tilda affected a fake upper class voice, which Ember assumed was an imitation of her mother, "I am supposed to be finding a husband."

"Harriet said—" started Ember, and Tilda's attention snapped to her.

"You spoke with Harriet?"

"Yes, all your friends have been spoken to, but I only spoke to Harriet. I thought there was some connection between your disappearance and Miss Ashton."

"Miss Ashton?" Tilda asked, her brow furrowing slightly. "We move in the same social circles, but I don't really know her very well at all."

"And you are definitely not a witch?" asked Ember.

"I assure you I am not, but that doesn't stop the baron from coming in everyday and trying to make me do things!" Tilda replied, her frustration on full display now.

"What kind of things?" asked Ember, refusing to let her mind dwell on what this could mean.

There came a sound from the corridor outside, a door opening perhaps, then footsteps. *Several people*, thought Ember. The light in the chamber dimmed and flickered as shapes passed by the candles and then brightened as if more were being lit.

A key scraped in the lock and the door swung inwards. Ember launched to her feet and ran at the bodies. She felt strong hands clamp onto her arms and realised she was held by a large man. She wouldn't be able to get free from him.

"Young ladies are all so impetuous," said the baron, sounding amused. "Don't worry, I will soon have you trained like my pet here." He gestured to Tilda who hadn't moved.

The man holding Ember pushed her into the middle of the room before letting her go. She stumbled in the dirt and he moved to stand across the entrance, his arms folded. A third man—the steward who had caught her snooping around—was holding two chairs. Ember briefly wondered what time it was, maybe the early hours of the morning, but it depended on how long she had been unconscious for.

At the baron's instruction, the steward placed the chairs down facing each other. "Tie them up," he commanded.

Ember struggled as the man grabbed her elbows from behind. "You can't do this," she shouted. "Lady Peyton—"

"Has been taken care off," answered the baron smoothly, causing Ember to struggle even harder against the steward.

"What have you done to her? She had better not be—"

"Be what?" he asked. "She will be fine in a few days, but her reputation might not be."

Ember aimed a kick at the steward with the heel of her dancing slipper, but they were soft and hardly had any effect, except for making him tighten his grip on her arms. Ember groaned inwardly.

"There are others who know where I am." she retorted.

"Who? A cripple and a dying man?" the baron laughed. "Did you not think I know all about you? Oh yes, your support team is formidable indeed."

Ember tried to ignore the crushing weight of humiliation at the baron's insults as she caught Tilda's wide-eyed expression. She offered Tilda a slight shrug in response, but the baron noticed the exchange.

"Ah, did you think you were to be rescued by a shining knight? A handsome young man? A worthy opponent to take me on?" he gestured at Ember with a cruel smirk "As you can see, they are in short supply, however I think you still have the better deal. You might still be of use to me. But you, Miss Merrington," he spun back to Ember and spat, "are of no consequence at all."

By now Ember and Tilda had been pushed into the seats. Ember's arms were tied behind her back to the chair, but Tilda's arms had been left free, the rope just tied round her chest. The steward had gone to stand by the brute at the door.

"Now," began the baron, "it's time for another lesson, witch. Let's hope you can do better this time, my patience is wearing thin." He addressed Tilda, but she only glared at him, her dark eyes taking in every move.

"Your family line of witches ..."

"I tell you we are not witches," said Tilda.

The baron barked a laugh. "Much like this one," he indicated to Ember. "She told me she wasn't from a long line of famous demon hunters. Granted her powers are slightly more advanced than yours, but in short you are both very disappointing." Ember struggled to grasp what he was saying about demon hunters. "Now, let us begin. The speciality of your lineage is fire, so try and see if you can manifest it. Put out your hand."

Tilda started to stretch out her hand.

"Don't do it," cried Ember.

The baron spoke smoothly, "Advice from the hunter, eh? Do you want to show her what happens if you don't do as I say?"

He motioned to the steward who brought a candle closer, bringing more light into the room. He grabbed Tilda's chin and lifted her face so the hair down one side fell back, revealing a purple bruise on her cheek. Ember gasped.

"You monster," she spat at the baron.

He raised an eyebrow, his voice honeyed with amusement, "Now that's the truest thing you've said all evening." Turning back to Tilda, he repeated more firmly, "Now, raise your hand."

Tilda did so, her palm up.

"Now conjure fire," he commanded.

Tilda gritted her teeth and stared at him. "I told you I don't know how."

The baron thought for a moment then turned back to Ember. "Hmmm, actually you might be of some small use to me. You might be poorly trained, but you do have your mother's power." He gestured towards Tilda, "Tell me if she is a witch or not."

"I will do nothing for you," Ember fired back.

"Oh I think you will"—he moved over to Tilda and rested a hand on her shoulder—"if you don't want me to make the other side of her face match."

Tilda shrank her head into her neck to try and get away from him as he raised his hand.

"All right, I'll do it," Ember blurted.

The baron's mouth formed a cruel smile. "I don't see why ladies insist on being so stubborn, if you were just more compliant we would all get along much better." Ember didn't think she hated anyone as much as he hated him at that moment. She vowed that if she found a way out of the situation, she would get him back for this.

"Go on then." The baron sounded impatient.

Ember took a few deep breaths and tried to calm her mind. She kept her eyes on Tilda but sent her senses out. With the baron she felt his impenetrable wall, and he smiled at her knowing she was there but couldn't push through. She checked the rest of the room—the brute was just a brute, hired muscle, but she could feel something in the steward. In her mind she caught the glimpse of a ugly creature, possibly a shifter. She shuddered and turned her attention to Tilda. There was nothing, and she was about to say so when she felt something. She didn't recognise it—it was power and fire and shadow—but it felt like it was contained in a bubble. Tilda was watching her closely. Ember blinked slowly at her, then lied, "I cannot feel anything from her, she is no witch."

The baron looked angry, and Ember feared he was going to strike Tilda, or even herself, but he stopped and clenched his fists by his sides.

"So much wasted time, time I *don't* have."

"I did tell you I wasn't a witch," sneered Tilda. The baron spun at her and swung out, catching her on the side of her head. Tilda's head rocked sideways and she cried out.

"Leave her be," shouted Ember, straining against the ropes that held her. *Helpless once again*, she thought.

The baron turned on her. "Foolish girl, thinking you could come after me." As he raised his hand to strike her too, she saw the low light glint off the dark stone in his ring. Ember felt her teeth rattle, her head spun, then the stinging started, and she felt a warm trickle of blood run down her cheek.

The baron stalked towards the door. "Come, we still have guests to attend to."

"Shall we untie them sir?" the steward asked.

"No, leave them. Once I have gotten rid of everyone, we will be back. At dawn we will dump their bodies in the river, and they will make a nice meal for a river creature."

The baron stalked out of the room without another glance, and Ember and Tilda were left in silence and near darkness again. The brute had locked the door on his way out.

"Tilda?" Ember asked softly.

Tilda slowly lifted her head, working her neck slightly

and wincing. "I'll live. Well, at least until they come back to kill us. I admit, I am not thinking much of your rescue attempt."

"I'm sorry," replied Ember. If she were being honest, she wasn't thinking much of her attempt either.

"Was it true what you said to him?" asked Tilda. "That I wasn't a witch?"

"Not entirely," replied Ember. "I could sense something, but it appeared to be blocked, like it was in a bubble inside of you."

"Oh," replied Tilda thoughtfully. "So am I a witch?" "I honestly don't know. It is not something I understand, but right now we need to find a way out." Ember pulled at her bindings, giving a frustrated tug of her arms.

"How much time do you think we have before they come back?"

"I don't know but we had better get moving—that steward is a demon."

"Moving, how?" asked Tilda incredulously. "We are tied to chairs, in a locked room somewhere under his house."

"Can you untie yourself?" Ember asked, as Tilda had her hands free. Tilda tried reaching her hands behind her but couldn't manage it.

"No, I can't reach the knots."

Ember shuffled her chair round so her back was to Tilda. "Can you untie me?" Tilda's fingers slipped over the knots and one of her nails caught Ember's wrist. "Ow!"

"Sorry, I can hardly see what I am doing."

A few moments later, Ember felt the rope fall from her arms. She briefly rubbed her wrists to encourage the blood flow back into them, then she untied Tilda, the coarse rope hurting and bending her nails.

Once free, Tilda rushed to the door and looked out

through the bars. "I cannot see anyone," she said, "but how will we get out?"

Ember pulled up her skirt and retrieved her lock picks and dagger. "Their first mistake was assuming we were weak, stupid women. Let's hope their second was to leave the whole level unguarded. You keep watch." Ember knelt down in front of the door and started to work on unpicking the lock.

"How's it going?" hissed Tilda a few minutes later.

"Quicker if you kept quiet," Ember retorted in a loud whisper. A few seconds later, with a final click, the lock slid open.

Tilda twisted the handle and the door swung inwards. The corridor ended just to the left of the door, so the only route was the direction the baron and his men had gone. The tunnel was empty but they crept along until it ended at a T-junction. The corridors extended both ways, ending at a door at each end.

"Which way?" whispered Tilda.

"I wasn't awake for the journey down here," Ember shrugged. "But let's try this way," she gestured to the right and they immediately started to move.

As they made their way down the corridor, the door at the end started to open. Ember froze, causing Tilda to crunch into her back. The steward appeared through the door, carrying two buckets with liquid sloshing over the rims.

"Quick, the other way." Ember turned as quickly as her flimsy shoes would allow, pushing Tilda in front of her. She shot a look over her shoulder just in time to see the buckets clatter to the floor, and in place of the steward was a hideous beast, crouching on all fours like a large wolf. The hideous creature was mostly hairless, with only a few bristles on its grey skin, and slaver dripped from its jaws full of sharp teeth. It sprung forward and a deep growl rumbled in its throat.

"Faster," breathed Ember,

"Obviously," Tilda said through gritted teeth though she sped up a little.

Ember shot another look behind her and realised it was gaining on them. Running out of options, she threw her dagger, not waiting to see if it had hit its mark, but heard a wet thunk and a howl. They ran as fast as they could along the passage, reaching a door at the end. It was unlocked and they bowled through it. In the centre was a large hole, a hatchway which had been left open. They both tried to stop, but skidded on the wet cobbles, straight into the darkness below.

Chapter Fourteen

"Ewww, that's freezing!" exclaimed Ember as the water came halfway to her knees, soaking her feet and the bottom portion of her dress.

A second later Tilda landed beside her, splashing her with the same water. Ember grabbed Tilda as she stumbled, preventing her from slipping and going under the chilly water.

Tilda sniffed, "I don't think this is just water." They both nearly gagged.

"Urgh, we must be in the sewer system, but at least there should be a way out." Ember looked up at the hole they had fallen through. "I wasn't sure I got that thing, but it doesn't look like we were followed."

"What was it?" Tilda asked.

"Your worst nightmare fed to the devil," replied Ember, unable to shake the image of the awful creature from her mind.

Both ladies watched as something rather unsavoury floated past. "There does seem to be a general flow to this stuff, so let's go in the same direction. I remember reading that there are inspection chambers somewhere along the routes."

Ember set off with Tilda following, their sodden dresses making every step harder as they waded through the mire. Ember was trying not to think of the lovely bath she had enjoyed at Lyndon Lodge a few hours earlier. She would give anything to be there now, soaking in warm, clean scented water. She wondered what the baron had meant by Lady Peyton had been taken care of, she hoped she really was safe and that nothing had happened to her, or her father and Daniel. The baron seemed to know a lot about her, but he seemed to know a lot more about her mother. She pushed the things he had said about her mother to the back of her mind for now—something to unpack when she had more time. She also had a few questions of her own to ask of her father.

The sewer section ended at a junction with a wider tunnel, and there was a small step down. The water in the larger tunnel was lower, so it was just swirling round their ankles, but it was still very unpleasant.

"Ack! What was that?" Tilda shrieked. "Something just ran over my foot!"

It was then that Ember became aware of movement along the side of the tunnel and swimming through the water, accompanied by unmistakable squeaking. "Well, they do say there are more rats in London than there are people," replied Ember. " I guess they have to live somewhere."

"Well, let's get out of here. I have no interest in dying of some rat disease. Which way?" asked Tilda.

Ember looked both ways. In truth she hadn't much of a clue, but was willing to own up to that.

"I am not sure. I haven't found it usual practice to study the sewer system, though it might be useful to know if I ever find myself in the same situation again." She made a decision. "This way." She turned, still following the direction the water was flowing.

"Oh," Tilda mused with a laugh as she followed Ember, "do you not see yourself frequenting the sewers?"

"I am trying to break myself of the habit," Ember laughed back, but then more seriously, "after tonight, I think my very short lived career in demon hunting is over."

"Don't put yourself down, Ember. You did get me out of there," Tilda pointed out with a warm smile.

Ember sighed. "I got myself found out, got captured, both of us were hit, we were chased by a monster, and now we are several metres below London standing in excrement and rat infested water. Not really the glorious outcome I had hoped for."

Tilda looked straight at her, "I will take a filthy sewer over being locked up a second longer with that devil. It was *his* choice to hit us. Not your fault, okay?"

Ember nodded and Tilda continued, "Thank you for coming to get me. I can only imagine that he meant what he said about us being food for the fishes."

With a smile and dramatic bow, Ember replied, "You're welcome, Lady Margaret Berthilda Fordingworth." Then she straightened and saluted, "Anytime you need a tour of the sewers, I'm your gal."

At the sound of Tilda's infectious laughter, Ember couldn't help but feel some of her worries ease, despite their current circumstances. "Good, I shall ask for you whenever I need a guide to the subterranean filth. Though remind me, when I next decide to venture into the sewers to wear more suitable attire."

"I shall make sure I list it as essential on the guide booklet," Ember replied with a laugh of her own.

Tilda broke into a wide grin before linking her arm

through Ember's as they continued walking. Her warm laugh made Ember feel something she had never had before—a kinship, solidarity, a friendship. She had never had another girl for her friend, it had only been her mother, her father, and Sam. She hoped that when they got out of this mess, Tilda could be a friend, though she seriously doubted it. Tilda lived in a completely different level of society to herself, and the classes did not mix. She would go back to her la-di-da friends and Ember would go back to caring for her father and worrying where their next meal came from. She sighed a little at the thought.

Tilda's hand clamping on her arm drew her out of her reverie and she followed Tilda's gaze. A shadow moved across the curve of the tunnel ahead. A huge, hulking shadow. Something was coming.

Ember looked around—if they went back the way they had come, the creature would see them as soon as it rounded the corner. Ember cast around, trying not to panic that they had avoided one danger just to run into another one. Just ahead, Ember saw a small tunnel set a few feet up the wall. Taking Tilda's hand, she pulled her forward.

"In there, quick," she hissed.

"I don't think it's big enough," Tilda whispered.

"It's going to have to be. I used my only dagger back at the baron's house, hiding is our only option."

Tilda hoisted herself into the hole. It wasn't big enough to sit up in, so Ember squeezed in beside her and both girls lay down, hardly daring to look. They shuffled backwards so they were a few feet from the entrance.

A sloshing noise echoed down the tunnel as the creature lumbered closer. When it drew level with the entrance to their hideout it stopped, scanning the floor as if looking for something. Ember felt Tilda's nails dig into her arm.

The creature grunted and bent down, and Ember tensed, her heart thundering in her ears. There was a loud squeak and it straightened up, a rat clutched in its talons. It lifted the rodent to its jaws and bit the head off before moving off again.

Neither girl dared move for several minutes. It was Tilda who spoke first. "Did I just see that?" she whispered.

"Yes, pretty sure we didn't dream that up. C'mon, we need to get out of here fast."

They clambered out of the small tunnel and continued, now in a more sombre mood, reminded of just how dangerous the situation was.

A couple hundred yards later they came to a chamber in the tunnel. It was circular and about ten feet in diameter. Attached to the side was a ladder, or rather iron rungs set into the brickwork. They led up a shaft to an iron cover directly above them.

Ember looked at Tilda and raised an eyebrow, "We may get out alive yet."

Ember started up the ladder, and Tilda began to follow, but as Ember cleared the water it started to drip off her dress, causing Tilda to hang back a little.

Ember reached the top and holding onto the top rung, she pushed with the other hand. Nothing happened. She tried again, and it lifted slightly before clanging down again.

"Are you all right?" called Tilda.

"It's very heavy," replied Ember, trying to keep the frustration from her voice. They had come so far for this to be the end. "Hold on." She climbed up a couple more rungs until her head was bent over and the back of it was against the cover. Leaning against the ladder, she used both hands and her head to push the cover up. It lifted far enough for her to slide it to the side.

"Come on up," she called down to Tilda and scrambled up.

Tilda's head appeared above the shaft a few moments later and she climbed out over the edge. Together they heaved the heavy cover back into place and stood up. The sky was just lightening to dawn. They both shivered, a combination of the early morning air and being dressed just in flimsy drenched ball gowns. Ember peered round her, trying to get her bearings in the half light. "I think we need to go this way, we are about a mile from my house."

They soon reached a junction and Ember started to head right, but Tilda stopped her. "Where do you live?" she asked.

Ember hung her head slightly. *This is where she remembers she is better than me and I am an upstart. Oh well,* she thought and drew herself up slightly. "Red Lion Street, Clerkenwell, my father owns a bookshop." Tilda nodded and hooking her arm again around Ember's stated, "Then we go this way, it is not far to my house."

"But my father …" protested Ember.

"Will be informed of where you are," Tilda said calmly.

"But—"

"But nothing," dismissed Tilda. "My parents will want to know I am safe as soon as possible and there is nothing more I want right now than a bath."

Ember let herself be led along as Tilda continued, "Tell me, does a bookshop on Red Lion Street have a bath?" Ember looked for any sign of condescension and mockery, but found nothing but an earnest question.

She sighed, "It does not."

"Then you shall have one too, as you smell just as bad as I do." Tilda gave Ember a small shove with her arm, but didn't let go of it.

As they walked along, Ember smiled to herself. Maybe Tilda wasn't the haughty, simpering fine lady she had thought she would be after all.

Chapter Fifteen

A piercing scream closely followed by a loud crash was Ember's first introduction to Tilda's house. Tilda had suggested that due to the early hour the main door would be locked so they had better enter through the scullery, which seemed wise, given the state of their dresses and the smell that emanated from them.

It was the scullery maid who they encountered first, and she hadn't expected to see Tilda, never mind in such a state. It was enough of a fright for her to drop the dishes she was carrying.

But Tilda had calmed her in a minute, then the housekeeper had appeared, and after the shock of seeing Tilda and the cries of joy at her return, had dispatched servants to rouse the household and to start warming water for baths.

So Ember found herself taking her second bath in less than twenty-four hours. She had allowed herself to be shown to a guest room and bath after first gaining assurances that servants were despatched to her father's house to tell him she was all right.

Ember had met Tilda's mother briefly, a stern woman, though maybe it had been the shock of being woken early and finding her daughter safe and well. But as Ember was being led to the guest wing, she heard Tilda being upbraided for getting herself in such a situation.

Ember luxuriated for a few more moments. She was sure she could still smell the stench of the sewers and wasn't sure that even a week of baths would be enough. Eventually she heaved herself out of the now tepid water and pulled on the clothes the maid had left her. They were Tilda's and they hung just a little loose, Tilda being of a slightly larger build than Ember, but at least it was clean and much more suitable than the tattered ball gown she had arrived in.

There was a small mirror above a dressing table in the guest room and Ember regarded herself. She looked tired and a little worn, which wasn't surprising, but more noticeable was the dark bruise on her cheekbone and the cut made from the baron's ring. It hadn't really hurt after the initial sting from being struck, but she did wince as she lightly touched the bruise. The cut was about half an inch from her eye and headed down her cheek. It wasn't bleeding any more, but it was a bit sore. *I wonder if it will scar*, thought Ember wryly. *Oh well, it's not like I was trying to use my looks to gain me a good marriage match.*

She left the rooms and trailed downstairs where a maid saw her as she hesitated in the large entrance hall.

"Please, miss," the maid said. "The family is in the dining room."

"Which is?" enquired Ember, unwilling to just try any of the number of doors and passages which lead from the hall.

"Just that one there, miss." The maid indicated to a door and Ember thanked her.

At the sound of raised voices, Ember paused at the door.

"What have you got yourself into now, girl?" Tilda's mother was pacing in front of a large fireplace. Tilda sat in a chair on one side and an old gentleman, whom Ember took to be Tilda's father, sat on the other side reading a newspaper. "Mr Benning called twice for you in the last week. What could I say? I had to tell him you were ill and indisposed so you could not see him. If word got out that you were gallivanting about with another gentleman, then Mr Benning won't take you."

"Gallivanting, mother!" exclaimed Tilda. "I was locked in his cellar."

"Nonsense. Why would he do that? You have always been a fanciful child."

Tilda blew out a breath. "I was hoping you could tell me. He mentioned my heritage, a talent inherited from my grandma."

Tilda's mother stopped in her tracks and spun to face Tilda, her hand at her mouth. "No! It is not possible, how can he know?"

Ember was curious and strained her ears to hear better. She felt there was more to this family than she first thought. "Know what, Mama?" Tilda asked, but her mother was muttering to herself.

"After all I have done to prevent this, to raise a respectable family, I will not have history dragged up. How could he know this? No, perhaps it is just rumour." She sank into a chair like a deflated balloon.

"Know what, Mother?" Tilda tried again.

Her mother straightened and set her jaw before rising again to stand in front of the fireplace. "Nothing, there is nothing to know and the sooner you are respectably married the better, and you are not to go anywhere without a chaperone, and no more dances for the rest of the season. You have always been more trouble than your brothers put together." She turned and stormed out of the room, sweeping past Ember who was still standing by the door without acknowledging her.

Tilda noticed Ember stood in the doorway and went over to meet her.

"I apologise for my mother's rudeness. Now come and meet my father." She linked an arm through Ember's and drew her to the fireplace. "Papa, please meet Ember Merrington, who found me and helped me escape."

Tilda's father put down his newspaper and smiled at Ember. She curtsied and said, "Pleased to meet you, sir."

He rose and clasped Ember's hand warmly, giving her a smile. "Thank you, we were very worried that our daughter was lost to us."

Ember frowned. It was a strange sentiment considering how little anyone had done to try and find Tilda, almost as if they had given her up for lost already.

The door opened and servants began to bring in dishes, placing them on a large sideboard that stood against a wall near the large dining table. They smelled delicious and Ember's stomach gave a loud rumble.

"Sorry," she automatically whispered.

Tilda laughed and pulled Ember towards the table. "Well as I haven't eaten properly for several days, I'm famished. Let's have breakfast."

Tilda gestured to Ember to sit opposite her. Her father came and settled next to Tilda as Ember looked at the array of dishes and thought she and her father could eat for a week on what was before them. She felt a pang of guilt that she hadn't thought of him for several minutes.

"Lord Fordingworth, please may I ask if word was sent to my father?" she enquired.

Lord Fordingworth inclined his head, "He knows you are safe and well and will be home shortly."

Ember ate until she couldn't fit anymore in. Lord Fordingworth had asked her about the bookshop and they had talked about some authors. Ember discovered they had a common interest in the novels of George Eliot and in mystery novels such as Wilkie Collins's *The Woman in White*. Ember considered the character of the very resourceful Marian Halcombe one of her favourites in literature, a point Tilda readily concurred with. Maybe despite their vastly different backgrounds, they weren't so dissimilar after all. But she was surprised someone such as Lord Fordingworth would give it any merit, as it was considered sensationalist, until he owned up to reading the periodical writings of G.M.W. Reynolds when he was a young man. Reynolds had been a creator of *Penny Dreadfuls*, which were still a staple of the bookshop's income.

"Papa," appealed Tilda as her father rose, "do I really need to have a stuffy old chaperone?"

Lord Fordingworth picked up his paper. "I am pleased to have you back Tilda," he said, "but you know I cannot interfere with what your mother thinks appropriate in how you behave. Perhaps you should give some thought to your mother's wishes." He too left the room.

"Urgh," sighed Tilda, slumping back in her chair. "Father means well, but he is secretly scared of Mama, and she doesn't care about me, she just cares that I stay out of trouble and marry well."

"What's wrong with Lord Benning's son?" asked Ember.

Tilda sighed, "He is at least ten years older than me, and I am suspicious of any gentleman who had not married by a certain age. He is already going bald and he leers at me in a very moist way. It is enough to put anyone off, but all Mama can see is his money, or rather what he will inherit one day. I admit being Lady of Highfrome Castle does sound grand, but I would rather marry for love."

Ember also thought that being the lady of a castle did sound grand, but she could sympathise with Tilda. She would prefer her own situation, that she would get the chance to love rather than be forced into a loveless marriage by parents. She sighed, knowing it was no use dwelling on such matters. She changed the subject. "I didn't know you had more than one brother."

"My older brother Earnest, he can do no wrong of course. He has already married and produced one heir, though he is only two years older than me and Freddie."

"And are you more trouble than your brothers?" asked Ember.

Tilda's eyes twinkled, "Not if I had been born a boy, but I wanted to do everything my brothers did, which is apparently not what girls should do."

Ember laughed and the girls continued their breakfast with Tilda regaling tales of the scrapes she used to get into, until Freddie went to Oxford and Earnest married and she was expected to behave like the other young ladies. Ember was firmly in agreement with Tilda that ladies should be equal to anything that gentlemen can do and how it felt like a constant battle against society's expectations of them. She marvelled at how lucky she was to have found a kindred spirit and how Tilda hadn't turned out to be the la-di-da society lady she had been expecting.

Chapter Sixteen

It was late morning when Ember returned to the shop. Lord Fordingworth had arranged for his coachman to bring her home. Tilda had wanted to come too, but her mother had forbade it and had engaged a doctor to check Tilda over after her ordeal of the previous week. Ember was pleased to hear that a doctor was visiting, the way Lady Fordingworth acted made her think that she didn't care enough about her daughter. Though Ember reflected her actions were probably more to ensure Tilda was still marriageable rather than any genuine concern for her welfare.

Ember entered the shop and there was her father, standing in the doorway to the kitchen. She paused for a moment, taking in the shop and appreciating being home after everything that had happened. She regarded her father, concern and relief playing across his face, and she realised how hard it must have been on him. She felt a pang of guilt at the worry she must have caused him. He knew the dangers with pursuing this line of work but she had naively rushed headlong into doing it anyway, without giving much of a thought to how it would affect him. She was wiser now, and her own relief at recalling how she wasn't sure she would see him again threatened to overwhelm her.

Not able to hold back any longer, she rushed towards him and hugged him. Daniel came through from the scullery, drying his hands. He smiled when she saw her and letting go of her father, she hugged him too. He stiffened, as if startled by her actions, but it was over in a second and he hugged her back, as if he was afraid of losing her too.

She turned back to her father and he had tears rolling down his face before a fit of coughing overtook him and Ember eased him into a chair.

"I was convinced I would never see you again," he choked. "When you didn't come home last night."

"But you got the message this morning that I was fine?" she asked, worried that the Fordingworths had not told the truth.

Her father nodded, "Yes, but I did not believe it until I saw you there. I thought it must have been a terrible trick."

Ember took in her father's grief, and then relief, a man both broken in body and in spirit, and vowed to herself that she would get the baron for making her father worry like that.

She knelt in front of her father, "I am here now, and all is well. I am safe and we know the baron was behind it all."

"What happened?" he asked, looking at her properly, seeing the bruise and the cut on her face. "Did he do this? I swear I will ..." He went to rise, but fell back coughing again.

Ember eased him back into the chair. "It is nothing father. It will heal presently and it is nothing to what I did to his steward."

"Did you encounter some trouble then?" asked Daniel, sitting down in the other chair on the other side of the fire. He looked almost as dishevelled as her father and she was sure neither of them had slept last night.

"A little. His steward is, or maybe was, a demon. I will have to look up which one, but it appeared to be a large hairless wolf type thing."

Daniel ran his hand over his chin, scratching at the stubble he had not had the mind to remove yet. "Sounds like a southern wolf. They can be very powerful—how did you handle it?" He sounded impressed.

"Well, I threw my knife at it. I didn't see what happened to it and then Tilda and I fell into the sewers, but it certainly didn't follow us."

"Tilda?" asked Daniel.

Ember cleared her throat, "Lady Margaret Berthilda Fordingworth."

Daniel's eyes lit up slightly, "Lady La-di-da?"

"She's not so bad," Ember grinned, remembering Tilda's witty remarks and how she felt so easy joining in with her. "Do you think the baron will come after me? He knew a lot about me, about all of us."

Daniel frowned, "It's a possibility. I will have someone posted outside for a few days, just in case."

Ember thanked him. It was some comfort that there would be someone keeping an eye out, but it didn't fully diminish the unease she had. The baron knew so much about her and she wondered if it would be enough if he did decide to take vengeance.

She didn't fight the yawn that escaped her. She desperately needed some sleep after the night she had been through, but she had something she needed to ask her father first. She had rarely asked questions about her mother. The expression of grief her father wore whenever she tried caused her to cease early on, so she was just left with her own memories. But she felt she didn't have a choice and needed some answers, otherwise they could all be in further danger.

She drew up another chair near her father. "Papa, please tell me about Mama?" she asked. Her father stared for so long into the fire that she thought he hadn't heard her, but she noticed the play of emotions across his face. At length he spoke, his voice hoarse with the effort of it. "She was the best of us."

Ember started to speak, but he lifted a hand to stop her. "I have kept this from you for so long, but there is no point now."

He shot a look at Daniel, for courage perhaps, and then staring back at the fire, as if he dared not look at Ember, he continued, "We were a team—your mother, Daniel, and I—but in truth, your mother led us. She had the strongest gift, the hunter gift you now also possess." Ember had heard this from the baron, though she hadn't quite believed it then. But hearing it confirmed by her father was a shock. "We were commissioned back then by the Crown, well Prince Albert, to hunt down the dreachen that had started affecting parts of the city. They had come through from God knows where when excavations started for the underground tunnels. We worked together for several years, and then you came along and Rose decided that it was too dangerous to continue while you were so young, so she let us carry on without her."

He paused to gather strength before speaking again. "Then there was a large demon hoard that was becoming powerful. Daniel and I knew that if we were going to defeat them, we needed your mother's help. She didn't want to, but we persuaded her. It was a difficult job, and we did manage to kill them all, but the cost was too great. We only just made it out alive and as you know, Daniel suffered grave injuries. Rose felt guilty that she nearly left you an orphan and blamed Daniel for talking her into it." He looked at Daniel, sad memories aligning his own face. "I am ashamed to say I did nothing to stop that. I didn't see Daniel again until he walked into the shop several days ago, and I am pleased he has forgiven me."

Daniel waved his hand, "It is all water under the bridge, my friend."

Robert continued, "After that, we concentrated on the bookshop and raising our daughter."

Ember squeezed his hand, unable to stop the tears from rolling down her cheeks. This was the most her father had ever talked about her mother.

"I don't think she meant to give it up forever. She was sure you would also have the gift, and I think she was looking forward to training you," he choked.

"Papa, why didn't you tell me this?" Ember implored.

"Because you are her daughter, you would also want to fight for what is right and I—" Tears rolled freely down his face. "I couldn't stand the thought of losing you too."

Ember hugged her father close and they stayed there for some moments. She was still coming to terms with what she had learnt. She was still shaken by the revelation of who her mother was, angry that she had never been told. Though she managed some compassion for her father for keeping it from her, as she knew he was just trying to protect her from the dangers of being a hunter. But most of all, she felt an overwhelming sadness that she would never know her mother that way. Eventually, when their tears had dried, Ember pulled away, and thought back on the events of the previous night.

"Papa, can I ask a question?"

"Anything you like, little flame," he replied, reverting to his childhood name for her.

Ember looked between Daniel and her father. "Have you met the baron before?"

Both of them looked at her, seemingly puzzled. "We have

never heard of him before this," answered Daniel while Robert confirmed with a shake of his head.

"He said he knew Mama. He called her Rosamund von Rhinebeck."

Robert's eyes widened and Daniel looked surprised.

Ember looked between her father and Daniel. "What is it?"

"Your mother was Rosamund, then when she came here, she went by the name of Rose."

Ember was confused. "Came here? From where?"

"Your mother was German. She came to this country when she was about your age."

"I never knew this ... how did I not know this?" exclaimed Ember. She thought she had learnt all about her mother and yet there were still more secrets.

"She wanted to leave the past behind," sighed Robert.

Ember was shocked. There was so much she didn't know, but some things were starting to make sense—her love of languages, her strange words. She needed to process this, but there was something more pressing.

"Do you think the baron knew her in Germany?" asked Ember.

"It's possible, I suppose," Daniel replied.

"What would the baron want with witches?"

"Witches?" Daniel asked.

"That's why he kidnapped Tilda, he thought her to be a witch."

"And she isn't?"

"No." Ember wasn't going to tell anyone Tilda's secret, that was for Tilda to tell and as she couldn't access her power, it made no difference anyway. "We need more information about why the baron looks so young, but is supposedly over 200 years old, and what he wants with witches." Her mind whirled; they were running out of time. If she had thwarted his plan for Tilda, it was probable that he was going to need to find someone else. He always seemed to be several steps ahead and it might be too late. She had no idea where he might look.

They all sat in silence for a few moments, seemingly lost in thought, when she had another idea—it was likely that given his age, he had done this before. Perhaps they need to look backwards instead. "What about checking some newspaper articles to see if there are any similar cases?" Ember asked.

Daniel rubbed his chin before nodding, "We could visit the reading rooms. They house the newspaper archive; it may help."

"Good idea, we shall go tomorrow," Ember decided, pleased he thought it was a good idea.

"You did well out there, Ember. I shall be reporting your success to the palace later."

"It didn't feel successful," Ember replied with a sigh. "The baron knew who I was, who you were, and we only just made it out. We managed to escape due to luck more than anything."

"Sometimes luck is all we need," Daniel smiled at her.

Ember suddenly felt very weary, the eventful night and today's revelations catching up with her. "I am going to get some sleep." She yawned and stretched. As she rose her father caught her hand.

"I never wanted this life for you, you know," he croaked.

"But Mama did," Ember protested.

"I can't let you go out there again,"

Ember turned back to her father. "I am sorry to give you cause for concern, Papa."

"I can't bear the thought of losing you too," he sounded broken.

Ember heard his despair and anguish, but she also knew that it felt right and was what her mother had been training her for, even if she didn't know it at the time. She felt the guilt, but hardened herself against it; she knew she had a job to do.

"I will be going out again, Papa," she said resolutely. "You are right—I am her daughter and I have to finish this." She looked at Daniel and held his gaze as she said, "But next time, I will be better prepared."

Chapter Seventeen

Ember lay awake watching the sunlight play on the ceiling of her room. She was so tired yesterday when she returned that she had slept right through the afternoon and night. She didn't feel like getting up yet, though she had jobs to do, her father to look after, and she wanted to check on Lady Peyton. But first she wanted to think, to go through everything she had learnt in the last couple of days.

Mother had been a dreachen hunter. A good one.

Mother was from Germany.

Mother had met the baron.

Ember sighed deeply. She felt like her childhood had been a lie. The memories she had, of a friendly and happy caring mother, always there for her, wanting nothing more than an educated daughter—were these the truth?

Her mother had died more than half her lifetime ago, and sometimes the memories wouldn't come so easily anymore. Tears slid down Ember's face; she didn't want to lose those, even if they weren't the full truth

Ember remembered some things that had come back to her in the past week.

Her mother had taught her to aim.

Her mother had taught her some breathing and mind calming exercises.

Her mother had taught her the language of the dreachen.

She already knew her mother taught her to pick locks

She felt fractured, caught between her childhood memories and the truth.

Ember squeezed her eyes shut, willing more memories to come, but they didn't. Sighing, she rose. She really did have things to do.

Sitting at her dressing table she stared at her reflection—did she really look like her mother? She had always thought her mother beautiful with her auburn hair and sparkling emerald eyes. Her complexion always seemed perfect, whereas Ember had more than her mother's smattering of freckles across her face, and her nose was too small. She scrunched it and then smiled, remembering her mother's brilliant smile. Ember thought she had inherited her father's stubborn look, but with what she had heard recently, maybe that came from both her parents.

She started to run her brush through her own auburn hair. It was a tangled mess, a far cry from the way Kitty had dressed it for the ball.

Another memory surfaced, a rhyme that her mother used to say when she was brushing Ember's hair.

Blood, it blooms the deepest red
   Darker than the hair on your head
   Look into the golden flames forsooth
   Only one will release the truth

. . .

Ember repeated it softly to herself. She thought she saw an image of her mother behind her, smiling and singing to her. Then it was gone, and Ember felt more alone than ever.

Mama, I miss you so much. Another tear rolled down her cheek, prompting another memory of her mother rubbing away the tears when Ember had been upset.

We can be sad, but we cannot change the past. We can only take action in the present to influence the future. Let's take it with both hands.

Ember smiled at the memory and swallowed. She rose; she really did have things to get on with.

❖

In the kitchen she found her father making breakfast.

"Here let me," she said, hurrying over to take the things from him.

"I am not so bad I can't fix my little girl some breakfast," he said, though he did let her take the kettle off him and sank into his chair with a grateful sigh.

"Don't exert yourself, Papa," said Ember, finishing the tea and making some more toast.

"Well, it looks like I will have to do more round here if you are determined to continue with this baron business." He sounded more resigned than angry.

Ember tried to push the pangs of guilt deep down into herself, but it did leave them with a problem. "Well, I have found Lady Fordingworth as I was asked to do, and I should get paid for that. We could perhaps get some help."

Robert nodded and sipped his tea.

It wasn't long before Daniel arrived, looking much more

like he usually did, having slept, bathed, shaved, and wearing clean clothes.

Ember was keen to leave, eager to start her investigation, but her father called out to Daniel. "I still don't like this, but she won't listen to me. Maybe you can make her see sense."

Daniel turned at the doorway, a smile on his face. "I wonder that you think I can make a difference, I never had an impact on Rose either."

Robert stepped close to Daniel, his eyes dark. Ember had rarely seen her father look so serious. Daniel's smile dropped and her father said in a low tone, which she only just managed to catch, "This is different. This time you are doing the training, you had better make sure she is prepared." Ember saw Daniel swallow and grip her father's shoulder briefly before nodding.

Then he turned to her, his smile back in place. "C'mon, we have work to do."

❖

Ember had been to the British Museum a few times as she loved learning about history and other cultures, looking at the artefacts and imagining life as it had been then. They hadn't had the money to spare to visit in recent years, but her mother had taken her regularly as a child. At the memory of her mother, she felt another pang of disquiet about not knowing who she really was. Ember sighed, but then thought back to their visits and wondered if any of them were actually training visits. She remembered looking at skulls of creatures and her mother seemed very knowledgeable on their anatomy. Oh how she wished her mother was still alive to advise her now.

Daniel led her through to a large circular room, which was almost completely lined with shelves full of books and tomes.

In the centre were an array of desks, with scholars and gentlemen huddled over them. There was a deliberate hush punctuated only by the rustle of turning pages. Ember also noted that she was the only woman in the room, but the others were so engrossed in their own study that no one gave her a look, something she appreciated. The newspaper archive was in another room off the main library, not quite so large but still big enough to take a dozen or so study tables in the centre.

"Where shall we start?" whispered Daniel.

"Is there any way we can find out about young women disappearing?" Ember had pondered what they knew already and was even more convinced it was likely that this had happened before. If so, then there may be accounts of the baron kidnapping young women, presumably witches.

Daniel headed over to a set of small wooden drawers. The drawers were long and contained hundreds of rectangular cards that he rifled through and then tried another drawer. Clearly frustrated, he pushed that one back in and opened a third. "Ah, I am thankful to the librarians," he said, pulling out a card that had *Missing ladies* written on it followed by a series of numbers. He showed Ember how the numbers related to the different tomes and then the issue numbers of the newspapers.

Daniel navigated the room to the correct sections. All the newspapers were bound in large leather bindings, and he drew a couple out and placed them on a desk.

Ember started leafing through them, looking for any head-lines that caught her eye.

With so many newspaper reports to look through, she saw a startling picture of sensational stories. She believed many of them to be the usual human vices—gluttony, murder, debauchery, and theft—but also there seemed to be a considerable number that were unexplained—disappearances, maulings, and beastly sightings.

She drew Daniel's attention to them and he replied grimly, "There is much more we don't see and much more that isn't even reported." He looked at the dates. "I do remember some of these though."

"You worked on these, tracking these demons?" she asked.

"We all did," Daniel replied, meaning himself and her parents.

Ember turned back to the paper, still not used to this side of her mother's history.

At length she found a few reports which sounded familiar —of a young lady disappearing, her body found a few days later. Ember shuddered and suddenly felt sick. The reports indicated that the victims' hearts had been ripped out of their chests.

Wordlessly she handed the report to Daniel for him to read whilst she swallowed a few times to fight the nausea. When she felt able she asked, "Is this him? Is this the baron's work?"

Daniel was frowning. "I don't even remember this case." Then looking at the date he added, "I was in India at this time."

They continued searching through the archives. Some reports were dismissed as the young lady turned up a short time later, some disappeared to elope, and some were never found, but eventually they stood back and reviewed what they had on the table in front of them. Five reports all dated from different time periods, all of them involving young women who had gone missing, and in two cases their bodies had been found with the hearts missing. The reports spanned the last seventy years.

"As dreadful as these are, are they the work of the baron? Surely he cannot go back that far. He only looks around thirty, despite what *Who's Who* says," Ember said.

"There are those who believe that some demons can live for a very long time, and some are immortal, such as vampires."

"I thought those were a myth," started Ember, then remembering what she had seen over the last few days added, "but you are going to tell me they are not, aren't you?"

Daniel nodded, "And there are those who can prolong their life through certain rituals and sacrifices."

"Like the hearts of young women," whispered Ember, a shiver passing over her.

"It's possible," said Daniel dully.

"But we still don't know if these cases are the baron's doing. No names have been mentioned," Ember said, though adding to herself she thought, *whoever it is though, I will find them and make them pay for this.*

She looked again at the reports, this time seeing past the gory headlines and looking at the details.

"The baron wanted Tilda because he thought she was a witch. Once he found out she wasn't, he was going to kill her, and me. It doesn't make sense."

He didn't say how it was going to kill us, thought Ember. She wondered if it would have involved the removal of their hearts.

She felt another wave of nausea and sat down.

"Are you all right?" Daniel asked. "You have gone terribly pale."

"How did you go after these monsters?" she asked. "Knowing how dangerous it was, not knowing if you would be successful?"

"As hunters we feel we have to. Just like the dreachen we hunt have a need to kill people, we have a compulsion to hunt them. Nature's balance I suppose, to right the wrongs. Do you feel it?"

"I—I just feel it is right somehow." Ember hadn't even admitted to herself how much she had felt this since the first time she had sensed a dreachen. She had thought there was something wrong with her, but she had said nothing.

"Even now, when I cannot fight any more, I want to. The desire is still there, and it is hard sometimes. It was especially hard seeing you go out instead."

Ember hadn't considered how it might be for him or for her father, but she had no words for Daniel. There was nothing she could say, no comfort she could offer.

She looked at him, but he had turned away, seeming to hide his expression from her. It was a long moment before he spoke again. "Are there any more reports?"

Ember brought her attention back to the newspapers in front of her.

"I don't think so, and none of them mention the baron, or anyone like him. When we were with him, he said that Lady Fordingworth was a witch and that he was trying to get her to develop her powers," Ember recalled. "Why didn't he just kill her, why keep her alive for a week? It doesn't make sense."

"We really could do with the Codex to learn more about this," Daniel replied with a frustrated sigh.

"Well, we haven't got it," said Ember. "So we are just going to have to work it out for ourselves."

She made some notes from the newspaper articles and the deeds in a journal she had brought with her, and straightened up. "We should probably go, we have no doubt taken up our allotted time."

Ember started to close the newspaper archive tomes for Daniel to return to the shelves. Closing the last one, another article caught her eye. It seemed wholly unrelated to the case they were looking at, but there was something niggling about it. She wrote a name and a couple of notes in her journal, then they took their leave. Ember was reluctant to leave the crisp silence of the reading rooms—it felt calm and safe, as if there was no evil in the world.

❖

The sense of calm continued as Ember walked up the drive to Lyndon Lodge. The noise of the main road receded as she neared the grey stone house, and the abundant trees were fully in blossom, framing the beautiful lawns. It looked a world away from the realm of demons and monsters.

As she started up the steps she heard a voice.

"I see you managed to escape then."

Ember saw Lady Peyton walking round the corner of the house wearing a wide brimmed hat and gardening gloves. In her hand was a pair of secateurs.

"Yes ma'am, did no one tell you?"

"Who would remember to let me know?"

Ember looked ashamed. "I'm sorry—"

"I am not talking about you, my child, but I will have words with young Daniel when I see him next," she said with a smile. "Now let's have a look at you."

Lady Peyton regarded her, frowning a little at the cut on her cheek. "Hmm, I think that might leave a scar," then with a little grin, "it makes you look rather dashing actually."

Ember couldn't help but smile back. "But what of you, Lady Peyton? I heard you weren't well?"

"Ha, I bet they told you I could not hold my drink. Well I was very careful, but I was drugged, I tell you."

"Drugged!" Ember exclaimed, unable to contain her shock.

"Indeed, come let us have some tea and I will tell you all about it."

Lady Peyton ushered her into the house and called to Dotty for some tea.

Once seated in the dining room and with a cup of tea, Ember wanted to hear about it.

"So Lady Peyton—"

"No, my child, please still call me Aunt Louisa. I rather like it and Lady Peyton is far too formal amongst friends."

Ember smiled, she would very much like to consider Lady Peyton a friend.

"Aunt Louisa, who drugged you?"

"Well, one of the baron's men. I think it was that odious steward as he was the one who was passing out drinks. I came over very woozy and sleepy, and too late I realised you were no longer in the ballroom and set off to question that baron, but I was bundled into a carriage. Luckily they just brought me back here."

Ember didn't let herself reflect on what they could have done instead, but even their treatment of Lady Peyton made her furious.

"So please tell me all of your adventures." She asked Ember.

Ember recounted what had happened and when she got to throwing the dagger at the steward, Lady Peyton clapped her hands and exclaimed gleefully, "Oh bravo, well done."

Ember completed her tale and the visit to the reading rooms.

"I just can't work out what the baron wanted with Lady Fordingworth, or if there is any link with the missing women."

Lady Peyton patted her knee. "I am sure you can work it out."

Chapter Eighteen

Ember stared at the small black chest on her bed. It was very similar to the one she had found in her father's room full of weapons, but about a quarter of the size.

She heard a noise and turned to see her father leaning on the door frame, his face etched with a grim resignation.

"It was your mother's, it is yours now." He nodded towards the chest.

"Did you ever intend to tell me about Mother?

His expression softened and he sighed. "I don't know, it seems what I wanted was a selfish desire to keep you safe. But this was your mother's wish." He crossed the room and placed a small key on a ribbon in her hand and squeezed it gently. "She would have been proud of you."

"Are you not proud of me, Papa?" Ember met his eyes and saw the worry he had for her along with the grief he held for her mother. "Always." His words were barely more than a whisper and he turned to leave. Ember fought the conflicting feelings of her father's praise and what it was costing him to see her walk this path, and took a deep breath. Looking at the small key in her hand, she asked, "Did you ever open it?"

Robert paused in the doorway, his hand on the doorframe. He waited just a moment too long before answering, "It can only be opened for the one it was intended for." He shut the door behind him.

Ember sat and looked at the chest for a while, tracing her fingers over signs and symbols she did not recognise carved into the wood. She thought it was black from paint, but it was a very dark wood.

Sighing, she crossed to the window and looked out. She thought she had known her mother, knew what her childhood had held, and knew her path in the world. She hadn't quite come to terms that secrets had been kept from her by the person she loved the most, about the person she missed the most.

She wasn't sure what opening the box would mean, or whether or not she was ready to know it all yet. A part of her wanted to, but a part of her wanted to cling to the old memories for a while longer. From her window she could see across the narrow street and saw that the workshop door was open and Sam was inside. She hadn't seen him for a couple of days and suddenly she wanted the normality of his easy going company. Placing the key on top of the box, she left it on her bed and went out.

She nodded to a well built man hulking in a doorway across the street. There had been no sign of any retaliation from the baron. Ember hoped she was beneath his notice, but it was reassuring to have the presence of someone close by.

Sam and Ember sat on a wall that bordered a park half a

mile from home. Ember had managed to get Sam to leave his machine for a while to take a walk with her like they used to. It felt like old times. It had been good to fall back into their own habits of teasing each other and Ember could almost think life was normal. Almost, because she felt there was something that Sam was wanting to say.

They shared a penny ice cream bought from a vendor in the park. Ember had no money and Sam just enough money for one, though he was letting her have most of it.

"What is it?" Ember asked, wanting to clear the tension she felt between them.

"Are you …" Sam faltered slightly. "I mean to ask," he drew a big breath, "Em, is everything okay?"

Ember took in the creased and worried face of her oldest friend, her heart warming that he had asked. Though he had always looked out for her and they had always been close, she had thought him so wrapped up in his machines and inventions that he didn't really have time to notice her any more.

"I am fine," she answered with a tight smile, hoping it was enough to convince him

"Bullshit," argued Sam, visibly angry. "Don't you lie to me, Ember Merrington. You think I am so focussed on my work that I don't notice the happenings of what goes on across the street—fine carriages, going out late, that gentleman is there a lot, you have a cut on your face. Something is going on!"

"I can't tell you," she answered flatly. It pained her to keep secrets from her oldest friend and it felt one of the worst aspects of this whole business.

"And yet you can involve me into making things for you that hold weapons? I am your oldest friend. Why won't you trust me?" Sam looked hurt and confused, his hair falling over his eyes making him look young and vulnerable.

Ember had the decency to look chastised. She had signed

the paperwork, she wasn't supposed to breathe a word of it to anyone. She sighed and reconsidered. She had now finished the job for the queen and Tilda was safe, so she could perhaps mention a bit of it. She desperately needed someone to talk to, not just about the dreachen, but her discovery of her mother. Usually that person would be Sam. "Okay, I will tell you what I can." She held up a hand, "But, it isn't much as I have signed the Official Secrets Act."

At the mention of that, the eyes of her friend gleamed and a smile tugged at the corners of his mouth. Ember knew that, in the same way as when they were younger, when she had scrumped a couple of apples from an orchard and ran to tell him straight away, that she could have no secrets from him.

When she had finished he blew out a big breath, "Wow, that's some adventure, Em."

"I know ," she said, then catching his arm, "promise me you won't tell anyone."

"Tell!" He exclaimed, his eyes dancing. "I want to join in the action."

"Sammy, it's dangerous," she countered.

"All the more reason why you need back up," he reasoned. "You don't have any now, do you?"

Ember groaned. It had felt a relief to have told him, but she should have known something like this would happen.

"We will see what Mr Beresford says," was all she was willing to commit to. They wandered back to the shop, Ember asking him how the ether vehicle was going and enjoying his enthusiasm for the project, even if she didn't understand the technology of it.

Sam trailed into the shop behind Ember.

Daniel came through from the back room and Ember was grateful once more that he was able to help her father out. He closed the door behind him as he came through.

"Your father is sleeping," he said quietly to Ember and then noticed Sam behind her.

"Is he all right?" she asked, worried.

"He is just tired, it has been a trying couple of days." Ember acknowledged that she had been the cause of that, then caught Daniel looking at Sam, a slight smile playing across his face.

"Oh yes, I believe you have met briefly. Mr Beresford, Samuel Hinton from across the lane."

Daniel's smile widened as he held out his hand to Sam, "Please call me Daniel."

"I prefer Sam," replied Sam, clasping his hand.

"You are the inventor from across the street? I have heard something of your work from Ember."

Sam beamed, "I err, tinker a bit." But he did look pleased.

"I have a confession," said Ember, biting her lip. "I told Sam what has happened."

Anger and surprise flashed across Daniel's face as he turned towards her. "But he won't say anything," she protested. "I know I wasn't supposed to, but I have been busting to tell someone and I can't keep secrets from Sam, he is my oldest friend."

Daniel crossed his arms and looked at them both, his face an unreadable mask.

"The thing is Mr Beresford—" began Sam.

"Daniel," he cut in, keeping his arms crossed.

"The thing is, Daniel, I want to help," Sam continued.

Daniel turned on Ember with something like fury, "This is not some children's game that you can invite your friends to play at." Ember blushed. How dare he insinuate that she thought she was playing a game. She knew first hand the dangers this role entailed. She opened her mouth to protest, but he cut her off. "You signed the Official Secrets Act, Ember.

Do you know how serious this is? Breaking that is not a joke, it is *treason*."

Her retort died on her lips. Treason? She realised, too late, she had been very naive. "I know, I know, and I am sorry," said Ember. She squeezed her eyes shut, and then remembering that she needed Sam, she squared her shoulders. "But if I am going to catch the baron, I need help."

Daniel gave her an exasperated sigh and turned to Sam, "And how can you help?"

Sam stuttered a bit. "I can fight, sir, and I can make things … weapons and equipment."

"Have you ever seen a dreachen?" Daniel replied derisively. "Do you know what it feels like to go against these creatures?"

"Daniel, I am going through with this and Sam will help," announced Ember. "So you can help Sam and I practise or explain to my father why you will not."

She had played her trump card and watched as Daniel realised what she had done, his shoulders slagging slightly with defeat.

"Well, we can't use the palace now that your mission is over so we can't do much training," Daniel stated.

Ember felt relieved that Daniel seemed to accept Sam's inclusion. "I can train with Sam and we will use the back yard until we can find something better." Ember knew it wasn't ideal, but it would do for now.

Daniel put his hands in the air as a gesture of defeat, but still looked grim at the idea. Ember sensed his frustration and hated that she had caused it, but couldn't help feeling that the odds were more in their favour with Sam on her side.

❖

The next morning Ember sat in the shop, staring at the

notes she had made in her journal. She thought back to the previous evening. Dressed in her training suit, which Sam had laughed at at first, but changed his tune when he saw how easy it was to move in, and they had gone for a run. Ember hadn't run much since she was a child, when she and Sam used to race each other, so she was out of practice. But she had enjoyed the rhythm of it and looked forward to going again. Afterwards Daniel had gone through some of the moves with a short staff, showing Sam like he had taught Ember. Sam picked it up quickly, then she had sparred with him.

It had felt good to be moving—especially as she was no further in her investigation of the baron—and she was looking forward to another session later. Daniel had arrived, but had gone over to Sam's workshop, interested in his ether vehicle.

Ember didn't look up when the bell over the door went, expecting it to be Daniel returning. She had just been thinking that a cup of tea would be a nice break from her study so she called out, "Just putting the kettle on."

"Thank you, that would be pleasant." Ember started at the voice. She shot to her feet, and in the doorway Tilda stood looking amused.

"Ah, Lady Fordingworth," stammered Ember. She was painfully aware of how small and shabby the shop and her home looked. She swung her eyes round it, seeing how it must look to Tilda and coloured.

"It is still Tilda, that is if you still want to be friends." Tilda's warm voice sounded uncertain.

"Yes, yes of course," rushed Ember. "I just thought, well …" she gestured round the room.

"I don't care who society thinks I should be friends with, I much prefer your company to any of my other friends," smiled Tilda. "Though Mother would have a fit to hear me say so."

At the mention of her mother, Ember looked past Tilda. "I thought you weren't allowed out without a chaperone."

Tilda's eyes sparkled. "I am going to tea at Harriet's. Father has given instructions to the coach to take me straight there and back again, but one of the footmen is rather keen on me, so I convinced him of a little detour so I could see you again."

Ember laughed, "I am glad of it, but don't let me get you into trouble."

Tilda gestured that it would be all right. "How are you? I see your face is healing—will it leave a scar, do you think?"

"It might, but there is not much I can do about that. It's not as if I have to rely on good looks for marriage."

"Well, I think it makes you look daring and men love a mysterious woman."

"Ha, I don't get to meet many men anyway," Ember laughed derisively. "And you? The bruising is fading."

"Oh, I could have a dozen scars and it wouldn't make a difference. Mother is practically forcing me to marry Marcus Benning. She says no one else will have me now. I had rather hoped he wouldn't either, but it is in vain."

Ember was glad she didn't have a pushy mother to decide her future. "Can you refuse him?"

"I am working on it. Anyway, my brother Freddie will be home from Oxford tomorrow, could I bring him to see you? He is keen to meet the person who saved his sister," she said, her bright eyes dancing with mischief.

"Yes, of course, but ..." Ember looked round her room again.

"Don't worry about Freddie, he shares the same thoughts as me. You should hear some of the tales he tells from university, such fun." Tilda sighed at the injustice of it. "Thank you, though I should be going before they come looking for me."

Ember smiled. She had been pleased to see Tilda again,

with hopes of having some sort of friendship. As Tilda turned to the door Ember spoke, "The baron might strike again as there does seem to be a pattern with young ladies disappearing. Have you heard anything that could cause concern?"

Tilda's face paled at the thought of it and Ember decided not to reveal the gruesome findings from her research.

"I have not," Tilda answered, "but I will ask Harriet. If there is any gossip then I will get to hear of it. See you soon." She smiled warmly before taking her leave. Ember didn't like the thought of resorting to relying on the gossip of young ladies to solve this case, but was willing to try any method necessary with so few clues so far.

Chapter Nineteen

That evening Ember and Sam went for another run, this time for a little longer. Stretching their distance, their route took them towards Smithfield Market. She loved the companionship of having Sam with her. She liked working with him and the training was going well. Whilst so far she hadn't seen any signs of retaliation from the baron, it felt good to be prepared.

Ember stopped suddenly near the end of an alley, grabbing Sam's arm to stop him too. She could feel a presence at the edge of her conscious bubble. It was the first time she had felt a dreachen presence since the baron's ball, and apart from meeting a couple with Daniel, this was her first exposure to one at large. She ignored her hammering heart, putting it down to exertion from running. She flicked a glance over at Sam, wondering how he would react and briefly regretted getting him involved. She decided that he needed to find out sooner or later.

"What is it?" he asked.

She shushed him and whispered, "There is something

there." She gestured with her head towards the alley. She stilled and sent out her focus. She wasn't strong or experienced enough to know what it was, but she did sense blood, a lot of blood. She swallowed, willing herself to not retch.

They peered round the corner into the gloom. There was just darkness, but Ember heard a squelching noise, like something was—*urgh*—feasting. She looked back at Sam who had gone very pale.

"What do we do?" he asked, looking like what he really wanted to do was run away as fast as he could.

"We go in," said Ember determinedly,

"I c-can't," Sam stammered. Just then they heard a whimper. "Is someone still alive?" he hissed.

"Let's find out. You guard the entrance." Ember stood up and entered the alley, keeping as quiet as possible, letting her eyes adjust to the lack of light though it was still too dark to see properly. She could sense that she was close though. She pulled a dagger from the sheath on her leg. A beast was crouched over a figure on the floor, it's back to her. Her foot scuffed some rubble and she cursed inwardly. It swung its head to look back at her. Two pricks of light shone in the gloom. It gave a chilling howl and she could see long teeth dripping with blood.

Ember could see a young woman lying on the floor. She seized as panic started to ebb through her, but it was quickly replaced by anger and the knowledge that she could do something about it. "You leave her alone," she shouted. The beast turned and began to stand. As it rose, she saw it was at least a foot taller than her. Ember gulped. It bared its teeth and slashed out a clawed paw. Ember didn't have time to think and jumped back just in time to avoid a slash across the stomach. It was scarily fast and she only just managed to duck under its arm as it slashed again at her.

She wasn't going to win at this rate and needed another tactic. She rushed towards it, diving to one side to avoid those claws. She felt a sharp jolt of pain down her arm, but ignored it as she had got close enough to aim a kick at the side of its knee. The creature let out an angry howl and she danced back out of its reach as it tried to grab her. At first she thought she hadn't done anything to affect it, but then she saw its leg start to buckle. She darted in again and kicked out at its other leg. Its arms had lost their force and she brushed them aside. She swung herself behind it as it sank onto its knees. She grasped at its head, yanking it back toward her, and plunged her dagger into its eye. She pushed it away from her and it slumped to the floor, dead.

She stood there panting from the exertion, trying not to think about what had happened—that was for her to process later. Belatedly she noticed spots of blood dripping onto it, and it took her a moment to realise it was coming from her. She examined her arm. She hadn't felt the pain for several minutes, so she was surprised to see the long scratch that was seeping blood. She wiped it with the rest of her sleeve, relieved it was already beginning to clot.

Ember turned her attention to the young woman—barely more than a girl—dressed gaudily in a red dress. She was scrawny, in need of a good meal herself. She staggered up, staring at Ember.

"Are you all right?" asked Ember. "Can I take a look at that?" She gestured to the large bite on the girl's shoulder.

A look of alarm crossed the girl's face and she darted past Ember. "Hey! Let me help!" But the girl ran on, past Sam at the mouth of the alley.

"Let her go," Ember said to Sam as she caught up with him, though she felt sorry that the girl had gone. She knew that for some women, their only option to keep from starving was to sell themselves. She was grateful she had never had to do that, but was sorry that monsters prowled the streets for such women. She turned back to the beast. It lay inert with Ember's dagger sticking out of its eye. It wasn't like anything she had seen before—humanoid, but with blue skin and covered in blue fur. She retrieved her dagger and wiped it on the pelt before sheathing the weapon.

Sam stood still and stared at the creature, his eyes wide at the sight. "What on earth is that?"

"I'm not sure, I haven't seen one of these before."

"One of these?" He focussed an incredulous look on her.

"There are lots of different types of dreachen. I don't know what this one is though"

"What do you mean *different types*?" Sam's voice was rising in pitch. Concerned he was going to be overwhelmed by the situation, Ember caught his hand and squeezed it.

"There are many different types of Dreachen that walk amongst us, and many of them look like us."

"Like us? How many have you met?" Ember squeezed his hand again as his breathing became more rapid.

"Hey, Sam, it's going to be okay, we are fine. I have met about half a dozen now and I am all right." She didn't add how close she had been to not being all right; right now he needed reassurance. "It is dead now." She gave the creature a nudge with her foot to emphasise the point. Sam's breathing slowed as he peered at it curiously.

"What do we do with it?" he asked, wrinkling his nose.

"I have no idea, but can you imagine the uproar and panic if it were to be discovered?" asked Ember. She hadn't thought this far ahead, not expecting to see and kill one out on the street. Daniel hadn't mentioned this to her in training and she hadn't come across what to do in any of the journals he had brought. But it was a problem, she could imagine the chaos if it was found by a member of the public. She wondered if there was somewhere they could hide it until she had a chance to ask Daniel.

"Well, I could burn it," Sam said, now looking at it as a problem to be solved.

"Burn it? How?" Ember looked round the alley. The buildings on either side were brick rather than wooden, as were the warehouses.

Sam smiled, his eyes gleaming, "You just keep watch."

Ember stood at the end of the alley, grateful there was no one about.

A few minutes later she heard a whoosh and looked round to see a blue flash behind Sam as he walked towards her.

"What was that?" she asked.

"I will show you soon," Sam answered and headed towards home, clearly lost in thought.

Ember started to follow, but not before casting one last look at the dark alley. Her previous thoughts of dreachen being nothing more than a myth were long gone, replaced with a kernel of hope that maybe she and Sam could help make London safe again.

Chapter Twenty

Ember stood across the lane from a small thatched cottage standing in a large garden. After she and Sam had returned to the bookshop last night and bandaged her arm, they told Daniel about their encounter with the demon. Agreeing that they needed to step up their efforts, Sam secluded himself in his workshop to work on his idea for dealing with dead dreachen while Daniel investigated similar cases, leaving Ember to follow up on a potential lead.

New houses butted right up to the cottage on one side, but beyond it the lane petered out into a muddy track. The village was slowly being subsumed by the expansion of the city, but the old cottage looked like it had been there for centuries. Ember had never been this far out of the city, so far from home before. Everything looked green, and past the cottage she could see rolling hills and trees, hedges and so much sky. It felt wonderfully clear, free of smog, and very blue.

She had gotten the address of the cottage from the porter at the train station. It was only the second time she had travelled by train. The first had been with her father as a treat, but she hadn't needed to use them before. Almost everything in her life was within walking distance.

In the front yard were a couple of small children playing, they looked to be about five or six years old. The garden itself was full of plants and flowers. She recognised a few, but mostly they looked like herbs. This didn't surprise her as she was hoping to see a hedge witch. She checked again at the notes she had made in her journal in the reading rooms.

Steeling herself she crossed the lane and entered through the gate. The children stopped playing, but mutely stared at her as she walked up the path to the old solid oak door.

The door opened to her knocking and an old woman stood before her, but before Ember could say anything, the woman cried in fear, "No, no! I don't want the likes of you here! Leave me alone. I have done nothing wrong." She started to shut the door, but Ember put her foot in it. The woman glared at her in response. Ember tried to keep as calm as possible, she knew enough that there was tension between hunters and witches.

"Mrs Bradshaw, please," began Ember as gently as she could. "I am not here to harm you, that is not what I do. I want to talk about your daughter."

"My daughter?" The old woman's hand flew to her mouth. "Is she okay? She has just gone to market to sell some herbs. No harm in that, is there?"

"No, there isn't, but it is not that daughter I have come to talk to you about," said Ember carefully. "I want to talk about Angeline."

She watched the woman's face turn from concern to grief, her shoulders slumping. "I can tell you nothing. I told all I knew to the police, and they never did find the beast who attacked her."

"I know they didn't," replied Ember. "But I think he is back and you might be able to help me keep other young women safe." Mrs Bradshaw looked at Ember warily, so she pushed a little further, "You could help stop others suffering the same fate as Angeline."

Mrs Bradshaw swallowed, her grief written all over her face, but she relaxed her hold on the door. "I don't think I can tell you any more than I told the police, but I will try if it will help." She called to the two young children in the garden. "Here's a shilling, go down to the shop and get me some flour and a bag of bonbons for yourselves. Make sure to bring me back the change," she hollered after them as they ran out of the gate with glee.

"They are my Cynthia's children," she explained, "my other daughter. I wasn't lying that she will be back soon," she said sharply and Ember understood the message, nodding her understanding. "I won't ask you inside, if that's okay." Mrs Bradshaw tried to sound polite, "But we can sit here on this bench."

Ember understood that the old woman wouldn't be comfortable asking a hunter into her house. She hadn't really expected Mrs Bradshaw to agree to talk to her, but she had hoped she would.

Mrs Bradshaw settled herself onto the bench and motioned for Ember to sit. "Now, what do you want to know?" she asked. Ember asked that she tell her all she could remember about the last few weeks of Angeline's life. As she told her story, Ember sensed it was a relief to be able to tell it to someone who wouldn't shy away from the reality of demons, even if they were supposed to be on opposing sides. Ember didn't like the black and white of it—hunters against all the demons, witches, shifters.

Ember found herself reaching out and holding the woman's hand as she recounted the final days of Angelines' life.

Mrs Bradshaw said something which sounded familiar, "She was so sure of herself, that Lord Montford loved her. I remember her saying 'I will be immortal, and he will hold me in his heart forever.'" Mrs Bradshaw let the tears roll down her face. "Of course he wasn't harmed when they were attacked by that beast that killed her, there wasn't a scratch on him. Not enough of a gentleman to try and protect my Angeline."

This is what had drawn Ember's attention to the story in the newspaper. She was sure there was more to it than a beast attack.

"Did Lord Montford come and see you after the attack?"

"No, I have never met him. I heard he went to Europe shortly after."

Ember's mind was whirring, but she asked one last question, "Mrs Bradshaw, how powerful was your daughter as a witch?"

Mrs Bradshaw looked at Ember for a moment. She frowned but answered, "We are not a strong sector of the coven, so you can imagine it was a shock to see one such as yourself on my doorstep. But that's a strange thing, Lord Montford had said he could help her enhance her power to become more powerful, and I think she was excited about that. She was always ambitious, my Angeline." Mrs Bradshaw looked deflated now, saddened with what the memories brought back to the surface.

"Thank you, Mrs Bradshaw. I appreciate how hard this has been for you." Ember released her hand and stood up, the sound of the children returning along the lane. "You have been very helpful."

"I hope it has been of some use. I hate to see others suffer as I and my girl have."

Ember smiled then, "I hope to bring justice for your

daughter." She turned to go, but was brought to a halt by Mrs Bradshaw.

"Are you Rose Merrington's daughter?" she asked almost in a whisper, possibly seeing something in Ember's profile.

Ember smiled briefly, one that didn't meet her eyes, and nodded, "Yes." She could hardly get the word out.

Mrs Bradshaw continued, "She was always a fair one, Rose Merrington." Then with an affirming nod, mostly to herself she said, "She would have been proud of you."

Ember swallowed back the lump that had appeared in her throat. "It seems a lot of people knew my mother more than I did, but I hope I can at least be half the woman she was."

"You care, it is enough."

Ember turned away again, tears forming in her eyes.

She was halfway back to the station when she heard a pattering of feet behind her and a small voice, "Miss, miss."

Ember saw one of the young children running up to her.

"Please miss, Grandmamma said to give you this." The child held out a small pot and a note. Ember took it and thanked her.

This salve is powerful, perhaps not enough to stop the scarring completely but it will help. Thank you.

Tears fell as she started on her way back to the city. She felt overwhelmed by the kindness shown to her with this gesture, especially when Mrs Bradshaw had been so wary of her at the beginning. She hated the black and white of it, the notion that you were either hunter or hunted. She hoped that change would be possible and one day witches and hunters could work to help each other, despite their differences.

Chapter Twenty-One

Ember was frustrated that in the couple of days since she had visited Mrs Bradshaw she hadn't got much further with the case. Even the bookshop had been quiet. But it looked like things were going to change. Ember didn't need any introductions to know who was standing in front of her. She considered his twin sister beautiful, but those same features formed slightly differently—the high cheekbones, the deep blue eyes which tended towards laughter, the full mouth with a ready smile, and black hair falling over his eyes—nearly took Ember's breath away. Luckily she had a moment to recover as Tilda introduced them.

"Please meet my brother, Frederick Stanton Fordingworth."

"Freddie, please," Freddie said and stuck out his hand. "And you must be the famous Miss Merrington?"

Ember put out her own hand to shake his, but he grasped her fingers and drew her hand up to those full lips for a kiss. Ember found herself staring at them, then noticed the mirth in his eyes and frowned. She pulled her hand away sharply and folded it back behind her other one as if it needed protection. "You may call me Ember," she said tightly, "but I am not sure I count as famous."

"Oh my sister hasn't stopped talking about her heroine, her saviour," he smiled while Tilda rolled her eyes.

"Did she also tell you about having to trek under half the city in excrement?" Ember countered.

"Oh she didn't miss a single detail." He still smiled and Tilda slapped his arm with her gloves.

"Freddie, stop it," she admonished, then turning to Ember, "don't mind him, he is insufferable."

Ember smiled in spite of herself.

"Tilda did tell me a curious story though." Freddie turned towards Ember. "That you can sense demons and witches and other beasties." The way he said it sounded dismissive like a child's tale.

Ember regarded him, "And what would you think if I told you it was true?"

"I'd ask for proof." He suddenly looked serious.

"She speaks the truth." Sam had entered through the door, Daniel just behind him.

Freddie spun round and spied the two men. "Lord Fordingworth," Ember began, "Samuel Hinton, my friend and neighbour, and Mr Beresford, who can also sense beasties, as you call them." Freddie looked at them both as if they were interesting subjects to be studied. Daniel had moved in those circles regularly so he didn't flinch, but Sam coloured slightly as Freddie looked from him to Ember and back again.

Freddie seemed to shrug slightly. "If you say so."

Ember ground her teeth slightly at his haughtiness and thought her bookshop was getting a little crowded. She didn't want her father waking as he had retired early.

Tilda, who had some grace, seemed to sense Ember's

discomfort and made to move. "Come, brother, you have satisfied your curiosity enough for one day," she said and started to push him towards the door. "Ember, I am having a small tea party tomorrow, please come."

"I don't think I can." Ember couldn't think of anything worse than having to sit and listen to a gaggle of gossiping girls. Not when she had a mystery to solve and a killer to catch.

Tilda put her hand on Ember's arm and leaned in close so only she could hear. "Please come, my mother is making me hold it to show that I haven't eloped or worse, and it will only be bearable if you are there too. Half of society think me daring and the other half think I have ruined my reputation. All of them agree it is scandalous, but only you know the truth."

Despite herself, Ember found herself agreeing and Tilda smiled her thanks. She bade them all good evening and swept out. As soon as she had left, Ember was furious with herself. "Why could I not have come up with a good excuse? I have got better things to do than sitting round drinking tea."

Daniel regarded her for a minute. "Sometimes we never know when we might be in need of some help. A friendship like that would be good to foster."

Ember was appalled, "So you say I should go in case Lady Fordingworth might be useful someday? How mercenary you are."

"In our line of work we cannot have the luxury of friends, Ember."

She scowled at him, "You are wrong, so wrong," before slumping down into a chair.

"What did you make of the brother?" Daniel changed the subject.

"Conceited and arrogant," Ember replied immediately,

which she thought was a shame considering how good looking he was.

"But did you sense anything?" Daniel probed. Ember hadn't been actively sensing, but she thought she could have felt something. Probably the faint tingle of Tilda's latent power. "No, did you?"

"No," said Daniel, frowning as if that was not what he had expected. "No, I didn't."

❖

It was growing dark when Ember made it to her room. She wanted some time to think things through. She felt sure she knew what the baron was up to, but not why yet.

Her eyes rested on her mother's chest, which she hadn't touched since her father left it for her. She pulled it towards her to have a closer look.

She ran her hands over the carvings. Some of them looked oriental in origin, some of them looked very beast-like—a tableau of horrors. It had small neat brass hinges and a keyhole. She ran her fingers over the surface before lighting a candle to better see the shapes. As she reached the part above the lock, she saw some letters. RvR. R could stand for Rose, Rosamund, but the vR ... The baron had mentioned von Rhinebeck—her mother's maiden name.

Ember tried the key, but it didn't move. She frowned and tried again, but it still wouldn't budge. What had her father said, or rather had left unsaid? He hadn't been able to open it. *Maybe it's not for me*, she thought, disappointed. She closed her eyes, trying to hold back the tears. She desperately wanted to see something of her mother's life, a life she had never known about.

There is always another way. She reached for her lock picks, finding comfort in the familiarity of the metal in her fingers. She felt confident she could crack this, but after a fruitless fifteen minutes she reluctantly conceded defeat. It wasn't a lock she had come across before and was too complex for her to unlock it with picks.

She tapped her fingers on the chest trying to think. After a few moments she realised she was tapping the rhythm of the rhyme she had recalled her mother saying.

Blood, it blooms the deepest red
   Darker than the hair on your head
   Look into the golden flames forsooth
   Only one will release the truth

Ember hummed the rhyme as she regarded the chest before tossing the key down in annoyance. Maybe the box wasn't really for her. Then she recalled the rhyme once more, wondering if it had a meaning. She always supposed it was nonsense, but given everything she learnt recently about her mother, perhaps it was something her mother had been preparing her for. With renewed enthusiasm, she picked up the key and held it over the flame of her candle until the key was hot. She tried the lock again, and still it didn't turn. She sighed.

She plucked a hair from her head and wound it round the key. Still, it wouldn't work. She gritted her teeth, refusing to let tears of frustration form.

Ember considered the rhyme, she had tried all the options. *Except one*, she realised. She considered it for a moment before reaching for her dagger. She gently pushed the tip into her finger. A bead of blood welled up, and she drew her finger along the key and then inserted it into the lock.

It clicked open.

Slowly lifting the lid, she peered inside. There were several books, notebooks, and a couple of daggers with ornate black bone handles. Laid on top was a letter addressed in her mother's familiar script, *For my Daughter Ember.*

Ember's breath caught in her throat and her heart tightened, a fresh grief at seeing something written for her by a mother who had been dead for over ten years. She forced herself to swallow, but her limbs felt very heavy as she lifted the letter out and broke the seal on it.

My dearest daughter,

I don't have much time left and whilst people say that we should regret nothing, I regret not having those years watching you grow into a young woman and to, as is my hope, fulfil your potential. If you are reading this, then you are already along that path. I am entrusting the keeping of this letter and my journals to your father, but I know him well enough to say that he will not give it to you when you are ready, but when he is ready. He loves you fiercely, like he loves me, and I know it will be hard to accept that his daughter has von Rhinebeck blood running through her veins, but I have seen that you do, my child, and it will only be a matter of time before you will gain the powers you rightfully inherit.

I am saddened that I won't be there to train you myself, but your father, although with hunter blood not as powerful as the von Rhinebeck, will be there to teach you.

. . .

Ember choked back a sob that her mother, for all of her predictions of Ember's birthright, could not have foreseen her father's illness.

I do regret not telling you of this sooner, but I hadn't planned to fall ill. Not telling you of your true heritage as a child was a hotly debated decision between your father and I, and as it turns out, he was right. To ignite your curiosity so young and then to leave you without my protection at a young age would be dangerous. Though we are hunters, there are those who hunt us as well. So the name von Rhinebeck was never uttered around you and we have put in place what we could to keep you safe, at least until your powers became noticeable. I am sorry that in that, your training will be lacking. I have done what I can with the basics and my daughter is a quick and sharp learner, so I know that you will not be at a disadvantage for long and your cleverness will keep you safe. But you know this as you are now reading this letter.

Inside this box are my journals, which will tell you more of our family, your family, and the work that we do. There is also enclosed a book which I imagine most who know of it think it is lost to history. Guard it well, it is your legacy.

I know you are beautiful, clever, and brave. You have all my love.

Rosamund, your mother

Tears fell freely down Ember's face as she pushed the letter to one side, not wishing the ink to smudge. Slowly she lifted the journals out, flicking through them briefly. They were dated and some went back even before her mother could have been born. A history of her mother's family, *her* family. She wondered who the von Rhinebecks were, vowing to find out.

One of the journals would not open. The cover was overlapped on itself, but she could not prise it apart. She put it aside to investigate later. At the bottom of the box—as big as the base of the box and laid flat, so she could hardly get her fingers round it to draw it out—was a large leather bound book at least a couple of inches thick. The cover was embossed with shapes and symbols, similar to those etched into the box. The pages were yellowing and there was some staining as if ink had spilled. Ember looked closer. *Maybe not ink.* She opened the cover and gasped. *Was this the Encyclopaedia of Demonology—the Codex?* In it were pictures and descriptions of a horrible range of creatures, more nightmarish than Ember could imagine. Some of it was written in English, some in French and German, and some in another language Ember could not decipher, Latin perhaps. But dotted through were some of the special words Ember had heard from her mother. No wonder she was so keen for her to learn languages—her mother had been training her, even if she hadn't known it at the time.

Ember felt Sam sit down beside her. He didn't say anything, just lent support. It had been a long while since she had climbed out of her window onto the roof. Years ago she would do it whenever she needed some space or time to think. Sam sometimes used to join her. It was something they shared as teenagers. She felt that need for space and thinking time tonight.

For a few minutes he just kept his shoulder butted up against her in silent support. She sighed, "How is it that you thought you knew someone, only to find out that you didn't really know them at all?"

"Your mother?" Sam ventured a guess.

Ember held up one of her mother's journals from the box. "Apparently I am from a long line of demon hunters. My mother hid everything from me and so did my father," she ground out.

Sam said calmly, "Whatever she was, she was damn proud of you, and she did what she did to keep you safe."

"I know, it's just a shock. My childhood, the time with my mother, those memories were my rock. The only time I considered solid and true, something I return to in the dark days, when I am unsure of my future."

Sam turned to her and smiled, "I think she has just given you a future."

Ember chewed her lip for a minute and then grinned at him. "Then we have some work to do."

Chapter Twenty-Two

"You made quite an impression on my brother, he has barely stopped talking about you," Tilda said as she handed a cup of tea to Ember. Ember took it eagerly, grateful to have something to do other than tug at her dress. She looked round the room at the other young ladies in the room, dressed in the latest fashions. The preference for pleats and ruffles, especially at the back, coupled with the smaller bustles was evident, and there seemed to be a dress in every colour imaginable. She noted that a few of the ladies were showing the newest design of bodice, cut longer at the front and back to give a sleeker silhouette. Ember thought it looked very elegant and repressed an envious sigh before turning her attention back to the ridiculous statement Tilda had made.

"I can't see why, he probably likes to talk about himself more," Ember retorted.

Tilda let out a low laugh, "He had bad influences at Oxford, but he is not so bad really." Ember raised her eyebrows at her friend, questioning her answer, and Tilda laughed again.

"I am not sure I should have come." Ember tugged at her

dress again—the one Tilda had given her after their night in the sewers. It was easily the best thing in her wardrobe and the only outfit Ember thought suitable for Tilda's gathering. "I don't know anyone here."

"You know Harriet."

"Hardly," Ember huffed a laugh, watching the anxious young lady talking animatedly with some friends across the room. When she had arrived, Harriet had made a beeline for her and thanked her profusely for finding Tilda. She had called Ember a heroine and how she could never do anything so bold.

She turned back to Tilda. "She is all right, but I have nothing in common with any of these ladies."

"I am sure you have more in common with my friends than you think, come let me introduce you to some of them." Tilda took Ember by the arm and started to walk round the room. Ember let herself be led, rather reluctantly, so she wasn't really paying attention when she found herself face to face with Felicia Worthing.

"Miss Worthing, let me introduce my friend Miss M—"

"Miss Duval," Felicia smiled and nodded her head in greeting. "How nice to see you again."

Ember felt Tilda's fingers dig into her arm—a silent question.

"Actually … it's …" A sharper dig this time. "Er, very nice to see you too, Miss Worthing."

"And your Aunt? I heard she was taken ill at the ball." Felicity dropped her voice to a whisper, "That she was rather overcome with drink."

Ember forced a smile, "She is well, thank you. She suffered no ill effects."

"I am glad to hear it. No doubt she picked up some peculiar habits from being abroad."

"I—" Ember was furious at the assumption and was about to stand up for Lady Peyton when she felt herself being dragged away.

"Come, I must introduce you to some of my other friends," Tilda interjected firmly.

"Miss Duval?" Tilda asked as soon as they were out of earshot of Miss Worthing.

"It was my alias for the dance, but it didn't work, the baron saw straight through it."

"I disagree. With the baron maybe it didn't, but I think it worked perfectly. How exciting to have an alias to hide behind." Ember hadn't really thought about it and was still contemplating if it was a good idea or not when she found herself in front of another couple of young ladies.

"Miss Anderson and Miss Claverdon, please let me introduce my friend, Miss Duval."

Ember sighed inwardly, it was too late now. She smiled and greeted the ladies. After another couple of introductions, Ember's face was aching from trying to smile all the time. In a lull she asked Tilda,"How do you do it?"

"Do what?"

"The forced civility, it is making my face hurt."

Tilda chuckled, "Practise, my friend, practise. You are doing very well, we shall make a respectable member of society of you yet."

Ember scowled at her and reached for a fresh cup of tea, but Tilda just laughed with a twinkle in her eye.

There was a disturbance in the hall and the door was opened by the butler who announced, "Miss Ashton."

"You invited Miss Ashton?" Ember couldn't keep the surprise out of her voice.

"No, well, yes," admitted Tilda. "Sometimes you send

invites just to have the right people at your gatherings. This was my mother's idea, don't forget."

Ember lifted her cup to her mouth and talked so only Tilda could hear, "I didn't think you bowed to social convention."

Tilda leaned forward and murmured back, "You are a bad influence on me, Miss Merrington," finishing just as Miss Ashton swept up to them.

She nodded briefly to Tilda, but looking at Ember she said with a sly smile, "I see you will invite anyone these days, your standards are slipping, Lady Fordingworth."

"Oh, I believe they are improving," Tilda smiled back. "Can I present Miss Duval to you?"

"We've met," Miss Ashton said darkly, then turning to Ember, "and you can keep away from Baron Monteray."

"I intend to, but if you know what is good for you, you would also keep away from him," Ember replied.

Miss Ashton's eyes glittered. "Jealous I see, but he has already said my heart is his."

Ember's attention snapped to the woman. Her words were just what Mrs Bradshaw had said Angelique spoke. Ember sent out a sensing tendril, which confirmed what she thought. "He is a dangerous man, Miss Ashton. My warning is kindly meant."

Miss Aston just smiled, "All the best men are," and swept away.

Ember leaned in close to Tilda. "Did you know she is a witch?"

Tilda watched her retreating figure. "I, um, no. Like I am a witch?"

"Yes, well, not really, she is quite powerful." Ember still hadn't been able to solve the problem of how Tilda was both a witch and not a witch. She knew there was something key she was missing.

"Maybe they are made for each other then," murmured Tilda.

"No," replied Ember, "I think she is in a lot of trouble." She looked worriedly after the woman as she talked easily to the other guests. Ember wished she could leave, she wanted to talk over her theories with Daniel as she hadn't had the chance yet. She sighed and looked for a seat, at least a sit down would be welcome.

No one else came to speak with Ember for the next hour and Tilda had been too busy playing hostess to have much time to talk to her friend. Ember reflected that though she thought her life was quite hard and she didn't have any luxuries, at least she didn't have to suffer the tedium of a gathering such as this. Next time Tilda asked, she would firmly decline.

She felt needed to make a move, she was achieving nothing sitting here. She sought out Tilda and caught up with her in a moment when she was alone. "I really need to go, but thank you for inviting me. It has been, um, most illuminating."

"You've hated it, haven't you?" Tilda didn't look hurt or upset.

"It's just not something I am used to." Ember wrinkled her nose.

Tilda smiled. "Ever the tactful, but I can't let you go home alone. It is getting dark, and there are monsters on the streets."

Ember laughed, "I know, I have seen some of them."

"Still," Tilda was not to be swayed, "I would never forgive myself if anything happened to you. Please let Freddie walk you home, if you can bear his company, that is?"

Ember laughed, "Oh, I suppose I could." She hoped he wouldn't be so arrogant as the last time they had met.

❖

Within a few moments, Ember was outside and walking briskly away from the house, Freddie in tow.

She took a few deep breaths, enjoying the clear air after the stuffiness of the parlour, and was very pleased to be away from the giggling and inane chatter about people she had never heard of and didn't care about. Freddie caught up with her. "You sound relieved to get out of there."

"Does that surprise you, Lord Fordingworth?" she asked, not slowing down.

"I ... err, yes, it does. Don't all young ladies enjoy gossiping with their friends?"

"I am not like most young ladies, Lord Fordingworth." She continued, "I have neither the friends to gossip with or the time to gossip in."

Freddie looked puzzled. "But I thought ..."

She stopped then and faced him. "What did you think?" She waited for an answer, but he only stared at her. Eventually he looked away, pressing his lips together

"I don't know, I have never met anyone like you."

"What?" she asked "Not met a woman who had to work for a living?"

"Well, yes, of course there are the servants and the maids, and well, I hardly think you are ..." he trailed off under her stare.

"That's the trouble, people like you don't *think*, don't *see* real people, people who have to work hard to put a meal on the table. I am just like them, I *am* invisible." A fiery rage was building in her and she spun round to set off walking again. "Don't bother coming with me, Lord Fordingworth. I will be safe. I am invisible, am I not?" She didn't wait to see if he followed, though she could hear him behind her.

Crossing over a street, she stopped and turned back to him. He was still behind her and had the grace to look a little ashamed. "Are you still there, sir? I thought I told you I didn't need seeing home."

Freddie stopped in front of her. "My sister," he mumbled, "I would never hear the end of it."

"Do you always do as you are told?" she asked.

"All my life," he replied, wearing a half smile that spoke the truth.

"It must be hard to do what is required of you," she answered.

"So you understand?" He looked earnestly at her.

"Sure my heart bleeds, sir," she mocked him. "To receive several hot meals a day, never needing to worry if it will be your last, to have someone clean your clothes, to bring you hot water, to never have to lift a finger, it must be a burden indeed." She turned then and stormed on her way, leaving him standing on the bridge. She was furious. *Insufferable,* she muttered under her breath as she walked along. *How can he think he has a hard time? I bet he has never had to do a day's work in his life.*

She was so wrapped up in her own thoughts and anger that she didn't see it, didn't sense it until it was almost too late. She was walking down a narrow street, a tall man walking towards her. Just as he reached her, he grabbed her and dragged her towards an alley. She had felt him, and his intent, a split second before he lunged, so as he dragged her backwards she was already reaching for her dagger. He was tall and powerful, but also sloppy, thinking that her slight form was easy prey. He hadn't seen her eyes as she had her head down, so he had no idea of knowing who or what she was.

He had grabbed one of her arms and as he dragged her backwards, he tried to get his other arm under her throat, but she was too quick and she ducked and twisted so she was facing him. In the same movement she had managed to free her dagger—a small part of her brain flickered with the recognition that the pockets she had added to the skirts were very handy indeed—and pushing herself towards him, she used her body to push her dagger into his stomach. Whether it was her movements that shocked him or the realisation of what she was, Ember couldn't tell and frankly didn't care.

"You made the wrong choice today, mister," she spat at him as blood started to bubble up in his mouth and he began to change into his demon form. She pushed him away and he fell backwards, knocking over some barrels. He sprawled in the alley, now looking like a large snake. She looked down at the creature, knowing she couldn't very well leave it out in the open. She wished Sam was here now. He had been carrying something which had burnt the previous demon. The creature was laid against a wall, so she thought she could shield it with a couple of the barrels it had knocked over, at least for now. She could bring Sam back later. She hefted them into position, grateful they were empty. She retrieved her dagger and started to wipe it clean, only to hear a gasp behind her.

She spun expecting more trouble, but found Freddie with horror in his eyes.

"What was that thing? I saw a man attack you, I was coming to help." Then the slow realisation of what had happened dawned on him. "Who *are* you?"

Ember stepped towards him, the dagger still in her hand, and his eyes widened as he took a step back.

"I am the woman who saved your sister, the woman who can take care of herself, and the woman who is going to rid this city of this filth." Until she said it out loud, she hadn't admitted it to herself. Maybe Sam was right, maybe she did have a future.

She looked down at the dagger, realising it looked like she

was about to attack him, she sheathed it before walking past him to continue home.

"May I walk with you?" Freddie asked quietly.

"As you wish," Ember answered, a slight smile playing on her lips.

<h1 style="text-align:center">Chapter Twenty-Three</h1>

"Do you mean to tell me that you had the book all along?" Daniel did not look at all happy. Ember had brought the Codex to the bookshop the day after Tilda's party.

"I didn't know of it," Ember started.

"I wasn't asking you," Daniel glared at Robert. "It would have been invaluable to us, to Ember. I thought it had been lost."

"It's not my book, it never has been. It was Rose's and now it belongs to Ember," Robert said in an even but very deliberate tone.

Daniel ran his hands through his hair exasperated. "But you did know."

"I suspected, yes, but the box was shut with a lock that only Ember could open, so what was the point of saying so?"

Sam sat at the table in the shop, oblivious to the argument as he slowly turned the pages of the massive tome, whistling at some of the images and reading out the names of the demons listed.

"The Vampire of Vienna, urgh. The Darius Quest, curious."

"Well, we have it now," Ember said as she paced the room, laying out her theories to Daniel, his face becoming graver as he went on. "I am sure the baron is the connection between missing women and witches being found with their hearts missing."

He looked ashen, "It makes sense, especially the timings, but what would he want with them? For what purpose?"

Ember caught a glimpse of one of the pages as Sam was skimming through.

"Back up a few pages, Sam."

There was a black and white ink drawing, a very good likeness of the baron.

She drew in a quick breath. "Daniel, come and see this."

The page was titled *The Blood Noble*. As she read the description, she started to feel sick. Looking up at Daniel she said, "We need to stop him. I fear Miss Ashton is in grave danger."

Chapter Twenty-Four

S am and Ember were out for a run, their third that week. Ember was finding it easier to keep going for longer and loved the exercise. She did get some funny looks running round the streets in the linen suit, but she didn't care, and as Sam had also obtained a similar suit, they looked daft together.

Also for the third time that week their run led them on the route past the baron's house and the club he frequented.

"Do you think we will see him today?" asked Sam.

"I don't know," answered Ember with a shrug. "We haven't been successful so far this week." Ember had been hoping to gain some indication of the baron's routine, but so far they hadn't caught a glimpse of him. It was very frustrating. She wondered if Tilda would know where he might be or what he had been doing. Ember had received a note from Tilda that morning that she would be paying her a visit later and found herself looking forward to it. She enjoyed her company.

They ran past his house and along the route to the baron's

club. No sign of him. Ember, not wishing to give up soon, ran a circular route that would take them past again.

"Look." Ember caught Sam's arm and they slowed down for a walk. On the second round past the Greyminder's club they saw the baron coming out down the steps, and with him was his friend Ashton.

"That's him, is it?" This was the first time Sam had seen him. "I thought you said he was young."

Ember looked again and realised that Sam was right. She was pretty sure it was the baron and he was with Ashton, but he looked older than before, older than her father and Daniel. The baron's face was lined and a little haggard, his black hair showing some grey.

Ember frowned. "I don't understand, the ball was only a week ago and then he looked to be in his twenties."

"Are you sure that it's the same person?"

"As sure as I can be. Come, let's see where they go."

They followed the pair of gentlemen as they took the route, now familiar to Ember, back to the baron's house. It was clear that they were having some sort of argument.

"I don't want you to see her anymore, I want you to break it off." Ashton looked angry.

"I have no intention of doing so, she is good for me."

"I will tell her I forbid it."

The baron laughed, "I don't think you have quite the influence over your sister that you think you have."

"But look at you, you could be her father," Ashton argued.

"A temporary setback, I assure you."

"So I hear. I think your methods are disgusting."

"Disgusting?" the baron sounded amused. "People like us cannot afford to be squeamish."

"I am not like you," Ashton spat. They had reached the

baron's house and the baron had started to ascend the steps to his front door, but Ashton still stood on the pavement.

The baron turned, his height looming over Ashton as he shot him a menacing look. "No, you are not." Then with a supercilious smile, "Your sister on the other hand." The baron ran up the steps and through the door, already opened by a servant, and slammed it behind him.

Ashton was left gaping on the pavement. With a thunderous look he turned and marched away.

"C'mon, let's follow him," whispered Ember, grabbing Sam's arm as she set off after the gentleman.

As they walked Ember sent out her senses towards Ashton. She knew his sister was a witch, but it didn't always follow that all family members were the same. She did feel something, it wasn't strong like his sister, but Ashton also had witch blood.

After a five minute walk, they watched him ascend some steps to a townhouse. He opened the door and they heard him call, "Severina, I want to talk to you," before the door shut behind him.

Ember couldn't quite believe that after days of waiting, they made a significant discovery. She needed some time to think. "What do you think all that was about?" asked Sam as they resumed their running and headed home.

"I don't know but I don't like it, Sam," Ember replied. "According to the Codex, the baron needs to consume the heart of a witch in order to prolong his life. That he looks aged in just a week could mean he will do it soon. No wonder he wanted Tilda. I think Miss Ashton might be his next victim."

❖

"What is it?" Ember looked at the small sphere in her hand. She was seated in Sam's workshop. He had called at the bookshop a few minutes previously with a smug but excited smile on his face.

It was round one inch in diameter, made of glass, and filled with a blue liquid. As Ember swirled it round in her hand, she noticed another smaller sphere black inside.

"And what's that inside?" She tossed it gently and caught it again.

"Careful!" Sam took it out of her hand. "It is an incendiary sphere."

"Incendiary?" Ember echoed, puzzled. "It can start a fire?"

Sam gave a self-effacing grin, "I thought it could, you know, help with getting rid of evidence."

"Sammy, you are a genius," Ember exclaimed, crushing him into a hug.

"Woah!" Sam pushed out the hand holding the sphere "They are quite volatile, I am still perfecting the mix."

"These will be so useful."

"You still plan on carrying on then? Even after you catch the baron?"

Ember inhaled a deep breath. She knew her decision would cause her father to worry, but now that she knew it was something her mother had wanted, she felt it was her duty to honour her mother's memory. "Yes, I have to, Sam. I can't stand by and let these dreachen get away with preying on the weak in this city. It is part of my heritage." She didn't add how the need to help, the pull to find these demons, grew stronger in her every day.

Sam was quiet for a moment before he looked up and met her eyes. "Have you told your father and Daniel yet?"

Ember sighed, "No, I know father won't be happy, but it's not my fault, is it?"

"Well, I will still have your back."

"Thanks, Sam, I appreciate that." Ember smiled at him, her eyes glittering. "Now, how about a demonstration?"

Sam grabbed her hand and eagerly led her to the yard. "Are you ready?"

He had set up a small area in the corner of the yard behind his workshop consisting of a pile of boxes and rags.

Ember nodded at him with an excited grin.

Sam threw the sphere at the pile. There was a bright flash of blue, a whump sound, and then a pile of ashes.

Ember walked over to the pile and blinked, then turned to Sam wide eyed.

"Blimmin' hell, Sam, that's fantastic. But I am glad you are on my side. Do you realise how dangerous this could be in the wrong hands?"

Sam looked grave and Ember realised that he was so engrossed in inventing things he never considered that someone might want to use objects to do harm.

"We just have to make sure they don't then," he said determinedly.

❖

"I think he is going to make an offer soon." Tilda pulled a face. "Imagine being Mrs Benning, urgh."

"Can't you just say no?" Ember poured herself another cup of tea. It was nice to just sit and enjoy her friend's company. Her father was resting upstairs and Daniel was over in Sam's workshop, having taken an interest in the updates on Sam's vehicle.

Tilda sighed "What choice do I have? Mother will never forgive me if I don't get married, and she keeps reminding me that she was already married at my age and if I don't marry soon, then no one will want me."

Tilda took a sip of her tea and looked around the bookshop "I envy you, you know."

"Me?" Ember frowned.

"You have so much freedom, you can do what you like, you can marry whom you like or even choose not to marry. You have a purpose. What am I destined for? Making heirs to fortunes and embroidering cushions whilst being bored out my skull with inane chatter."

Ember laughed at her remarks, but Tilda scowled, "You scoff, but it isn't fair."

"You know I have envied you."

"Me?" Tilda sounded incredulous. "What have I got that anyone could possibly want?"

"Oh, I don't know," smiled Ember, "maybe a warm comfortable house, a bath, regular hot meals, someone to do your washing …"

"Lord, I hadn't thought about it like that. Is it human nature to never be satisfied with what you have?"

"I have no idea."

"But you can't envy me the prospect of being Mrs Benning, can you?"

"No," replied Ember, "that I don't, though I am sure someone would."

"Great." Tilda's eyes danced with merriment, "Let's find her quick and I can shove her in front of Marcus."

They laughed, and Ember was surprised how easy it felt to be around Tilda. It still felt a little strange having a friend such as her, but she enjoyed the comfortable feeling she had in her presence.

Tilda said seriously, "I wish I could get to the bottom of this being a witch business."

"Have you told Freddie?"

"What can I tell him? Oh, apparently I might be a witch, except I am not because I have no power or any idea of what it might be. It is one thing to understand they exist but to have that within your own family, it might be too much."

"Hmmm," Ember hummed, trying to process the predicament her friend was in. "What about finding out more about your grandma? The one you said you heard stories about."

"I don't know, I can't ask Mama." Tilda looked thoughtful for a moment, "But I do have an aunt, Aunt Dorothy. She and Mama fell out years ago, and I haven't seen her since I was little. I will write to her. Thanks, Ember, I knew you would help."

Ember was pleased that Tilda might get some answers, but she was still worried about how she could warn Miss Ashton that she might be in danger. She relayed her fears to Tilda.

Tilda looked thoughtful for a minute before answering, "I think I know where she might be in a couple of days. I will enquire."

❖

"What do you mean?" Daniel glared at Ember, not catching her meaning. They stood facing each other down over the table in the bookshop. Shortly after Tilda had left, Daniel returned from visiting Sam's workshop and she decided to share her decision.

"If we are going to rebuild the dreachen hunting department—"

Daniel barked a short laugh. "Is that what you think you are doing? I am helping you solve the mystery of the baron, not take on the rest of the dreachen." He continued the attack, "And with what money?"

"I thought the queen might—"

"I told you, the queen does not support the idea."

Ember stared at him in disbelief. She had finally accepted who she was—who she was always meant to be—and refused to believe it was already slipping away from her. "But—"

"But nothing, Ember," sighed Daniel, looking older, like this was an argument he had held many times. "There will be no department, the queen does not acknowledge that there is a big enough problem."

"You know the pull of the hunter, Daniel, you told me of it yourself. Did you really think I could ignore it, knowing all this?"

"It will break your father …"

Ember felt a wave of anger rise inside her and her face grew hot. "Don't you dare," she said through gritted teeth. "All my life, secrets have been kept from me and now that I know them, don't try and make me feel guilty for what I am." She turned and stormed out, refusing to hear anything else he had to say.

Chapter Twenty-Five

"Will you relax?" Tilda leaned in close to whisper, "You look quite lovely, you know."

Ember exhaled a held breath. "I just feel so, so ..." she searched for the right word, "like an imposter."

Tilda emitted her lovely laugh. "We all do, but we can all act the part."

Ember looked at her friend and smiled. She looked resplendent and suited the elegance of the evening whereas Ember felt a forgery in comparison. Awkward of the situation, the borrowed dress, she felt that any eyes on her could see through her disguise and found her wanting. They knew she didn't belong.

Ember had never been to the opera before, had never been to any show, play, or the theatre. She had seen a few market-place plays on holidays in the parks in the city, but never something as grand as this. The Royal Opera house was magnificent, and they were in the Fordingworth box. Tilda and Freddie had arranged the details, and they were attending along with Sam and Ember. Ember had thought her father would have enjoyed the opera, though that wasn't what they were there for. They were there for the baron. Tilda had heard in her social circle that he would be attending that evening.

Ember sat in another borrowed dress as Tilda had declared that she really didn't have something suitable for the opera and whilst Ember had protested, looking round at the finery of every other person in the room, she had to agree. She had never seen so much elegance, so much lace and tulle, and the jewels that glittered on the ladies' necks, wrists, fingers, and ears, as well as in their hair—she could only marvel at what wealth there was.

The four of them sat in the box, and Ember smiled at Sam, who looked very smart in his borrowed suit. Looking at him, she realised he must have borrowed it from Daniel, as Freddie was a much larger build than Sam. "You look very dapper. Those clothes suit you. I think Daniel is having an improving effect on you." She smiled at him and thought she saw a hint of a blush, though he didn't meet her eyes.

"He has been very kind," was all the answer he would give.

Freddie lounged in his chair on the other side of Tilda who was seated next to Ember. He looked comfortable and at ease in the surroundings. He had been more humble since the encounter with the beast, but he was still, as far as Ember was concerned, a self-assured arrogant snob.

The opera had started and Ember tried to focus on the stage, but she didn't know if this plan was going to work.

"Are they sure they will be here?" Ember's nerves were tightly wound and she dared not reach out her senses anymore as she knew that the baron could tell if she did.

"Yes, they will be here," Tilda assured her "Be patient and enjoy yourself. This is one of my favourite arias."

Later, Ember wouldn't remember which opera they had seen, or any of the sound of it, although she enjoyed it at the time during the brief moment they were there. She tried to lose herself in the music—the arias were uplifting and the musicians very accomplished. She loved music, but hardly ever got to hear it and wished she was there under different circumstances.

Her thoughts raced. What if the baron didn't show up? What if Miss Ashton wasn't with him, or what if she wouldn't get a chance to speak to her before it was too late? Now that Ember had stated her intentions to Daniel, she couldn't fail at her chance to prove that she was right to pursue this. She couldn't face going back to the bookshop empty handed.

Lost in her thoughts, Ember startled at the light touch on her arm. She looked at Tilda and then followed her eyes to where she was indicating to another box across the theatre.

She shot a look over to the box and met the eyes of Miss Ashton looking straight back at her.

"Damn," she muttered, causing the others in the box to look at her. "I think we have been noticed."

She felt the faint shimmer of Miss Ashton's energy. Her power seemed to be a bit stronger since Ember last saw her. Ember frowned in concern, but it was consistent with the baron's methods. She knew as much from when he had tried to get Tilda to use her power.

Ember looked back and saw Miss Ashton whisper to the baron. He scowled and swung his head over towards her, looking fully at her. She stared back at him in shock—he looked younger again, all the wrinkles and greyness gone. He smiled and raised his eyebrows at her.

"Plan B," murmured Ember. "We need to move now."

She was on her feet in an instant, the element of surprise they had hoped for gone, and she only wished now they could get there in time. She sprinted down the corridor that ran behind the boxes, pleased that she had decided to wear flat shoes to the opera as they were better than the dancing slippers she got caught in last time.

She skidded to a halt at the door that must be the baron's box. It was closed. The others had caught up and stood behind her, panting. Ember carefully opened the door, bracing herself to face the baron again, but the box was empty. She spun round. "C'mon," she called over her shoulder as she started running down the corridor again.

She couldn't let them get away. She needed to do what she could to help Miss Ashton. She had no doubt that she was in danger now. Ember pounded down another passage, but couldn't see them. She sent out her senses and felt that they were close, and round the next bend she saw them. The baron was fairly dragging Miss Ashton along, her movement constricted by her tight dress.

"Stop!" Ember shouted, relieved at the sight of them, but the adrenaline coursing through her warned the battle was far from over. "Or what?" snarled the baron. "What can you do to me?"

Ember drew out a couple of throwing knives.

"I am a pretty good shot, did your steward not tell you?" She hazarded a guess that her shot had hit home and the look on his face confirmed it. He twisted Miss Ashton in front of him.

"That's not very gentlemanly!" Tilda exclaimed.

But he was whispering in Miss Ashton's ear. She glanced at him and then back at them with a wicked smile. She raised her hand towards them and a dark smokey substance started emitting from it.

"What is that!" Ember heard an exclamation, and thought it had come from Freddie. The smoke grew thicker and then moved towards them. Ember could feel a burning in her throat and her eyes started to sting.

"Close your eyes and try not to breathe it in," she said just as Sam started violently coughing. Ember tried to push through the smoke, but it felt like a solid barrier and she couldn't see anything. Sam was on his knees, wretchedly coughing, her eyes watered, and looking at Tilda and Freddie it was having the same effect on them. Then the smoke started to dissipate and Ember looked down the corridor. It was empty, but she could see to the door beyond.

"They have gone," she said, sheathing her knives. She felt a bit deflated, but refused to accept defeat. She was determined to keep going. "We have to go after them."

Sam was still sounding rough and Tilda was not looking much better. "You and Freddie go." She sounded hoarse. "I will look after Sam."

Ember looked at Sam who nodded confirmation, so grabbing Freddie's arm she set off in pursuit. The door led to a stairwell. She heard a door bang at the bottom and charged down them, taking several at a time, Freddie matching her pace. They burst through the door at the bottom and out onto a cobbled back street where they saw a carriage departing. Not needing the element of stealth this time, she threw out her senses and confirmed that the baron and Miss Ashton were in the coach.

"Damn!" she shouted in frustration, spinning round, her fisting hands down by her sides, needing something to focus her adrenaline on.

Freddie grabbed her arms, clearly fearing she might take a swing at him, and looked at her. They hadn't been that close before and she saw the light flecks in his eyes as they caught in the moonlight. "Can you track them?" he asked quietly.

Ember hadn't thought of using her power that way. "Yes, I think so, though I am not sure how close I have to be."

She focused her energy on the way they had gone, she

could still feel them. "It is getting weaker but yes, I can. They are"—she tilted her head a minute, trying to bring up a mental map of the city—"heading for the docks," she announced. "I will get there, you bring the others."

Freddie agreed and gave her a little shove down the street, "You go get them, Ember."

She set off running. She would never be able to outrun a carriage and horses, but she did know the city and knew a few shortcuts where horses could not go.

❖

Ember pounded through the dark streets. It was starting to rain with a wet mist, the cobbles becoming slippery under her feet. She ducked down a few alleyways, grateful nothing dared intercept her tonight. Her path took her through Covent Garden Market— it never slept and it was stocking for the morning trade to the wholesalers that would start in just a few hours. Her lungs were starting to burn, it was the furthest she had run at speed. She headed towards the river, past the bones of the building work on the embankment and towards the docks.

Seeing a carriage pull up in the distance she put on a spurt of speed, her focus now on saving Miss Ashton first and then stopping the baron.

She reached the end of a street facing the docks. She was almost there when the baron stepped out in front of her. She didn't know how he could have gotten there so quickly. Had he known she was there and alighted early? She didn't have time to work it out. Skidding to a halt, she almost collided with him.

He grabbed her, and with one hand holding her chin, he

regarded her. His eyes glinted and a faint smile appeared when he saw the scar on her cheek.

She struggled, trying to free herself, hating that she had gotten herself caught. She drew her head back to try and release it, but he tightened his grip. "Proud of your work?" Ember glared at his smile of smug satisfaction.

"Always," he replied. "But you, girl, are causing me some bother again."

"I know what you did to Angelique Bradshaw." The baron paused for a second as if he didn't recall the name.

"Lord Mountford," Ember prompted.

"Ah yes, what a sweet girl that one was."

Ember, vowing to bring seven shades of hell on the baron, tried again to pull free, but he was too strong.

"How many titles have you assumed?" she ground out.

"Too many to remember," he said dismissively.

"Who was it this time?" His eyes gleamed at her question, a smile playing on his lips.

"You work it out, *Targa*." He squeezed her jaw a little tighter. "Maybe I should have taken you instead."

"I am not a witch," she spat.

The baron chuckled softly, his silky voice chilling her. "You are an even greater prize, you are Rosamund von Rhinebeck's daughter." He turned her face slightly as if examining the value of an animal. "But you are not yet ready."

"Em, Em!" A shout in the distance and the sound of running feet. "Let her go, you brute."

The baron laughed, "I will be back for you." He shoved her and Ember stumbled backwards, her foot slipping on a cobblestone. She sat down while the baron whirled away.

It was Sam who reached her first, helping her up with a hand on her arm.

"Em, are you all right? What did he say?"

"It was nothing, Sam. I am all right," Ember said distantly.

She saw them step up a gangway and onto a small boat, its engines already idling, the hot steam hissing in the fine rain.

Ember knew she needed to try again.

"Stop!" she shouted. "Miss Ashton, you are in danger. Jump, you can make it!" The boat started moving off.

Both the baron and Miss Ashton were laughing. He motioned to the captain to stop the boat, just out of range for her to jump.

"You have lost, Miss von Rhinebeck," called the baron.

Ember appealed to Miss Ashton, "Miss Ashton, he wants your heart."

Miss Ashton gave a feral smile, turned to the baron and kissed him, before turning back to Ember. "He already has it."

Not like that, thought Ember. "Why do you do it, Blood Noble?" She chose to use his real title.

His eyes flickered and he looked gleeful that she finally knew who, no, *what* he was. "What everyone wants, power and immortality." He shrugged as if ripping out the hearts of witches was just something you did.

Ember barely registered the rest of her friends gathering behind her until the baron said, "Oh you can do better than this, Miss von Rhinebeck. Such a motley crew you have—a powerless witch, a cobbler's son, and a fop. Hardly worthy opponents are they. Too bad."

"Did he just call me a fop?" exclaimed Freddie.

"Shut it." His sister rapped her hand across his arm.

Ember tried another approach. "What about your brother?" she called to Miss Ashton.

Miss Ashton pouted a little in mock sadness, "Ah, poor Vincent, no, he didn't approve."

The baron gestured to the captain to start the boat moving again. "Until next time, Miss von Rhinebeck. I look forward to meeting you again."

Ember looked round for another boat, but all other steamboats were silent and it would take too long for the engines to reach enough steam to catch them. There were a few rowing boats, but they would never be able to row at a speed to catch the boat they were on. She watched with a sinking feeling as the boat disappeared down the river. Maybe Daniel was right, she thought, *I'm not cut out for this.* She turned away from the river and sat down on a crate on the quayside, feeling she had let everyone down.

Chapter Twenty-Six

S he barely registered that Sam was speaking to her until he practically shouted her name. She lifted her head and saw nothing but concern in his eyes. "Ember, what is it?"

She sighed, "I have failed. I've failed you all. Miss Ashton, Daniel, my father—"

"Are you really going to sit there and wallow in self pity?" Sam cut her off.

"Sam, I can't do this." Her shoulders slumped again and she looked back at the floor. Sam caught her arms and gave her a little shake. She raised her eyes to his. "Leave me alone, Sam. Go home, it's over."

"You don't believe that any more than I do. You are the smartest and bravest person I know. You never give up, it is one of the things that makes you, you. I know you can solve this, you just need to think." He drew her into his arms and gave her a hug. Ember drew strength from the comfort of her oldest friend. She took a deep breath, hoping Sam was right. She waited for her head to clear. She knew there was something she was missing. She thought for a minute. There was something that rankled her about Miss Ashton's words, and she spied the carriage that was waiting behind them. "Come on, maybe this isn't over yet."

They didn't speak much as the carriage clattered through the streets, but they all looked questioningly at her as they drew up outside a large house—Ashton's house.

"I didn't like what Miss Ashton said," Ember gave as an explanation. "Why would someone refer to their brother in the past tense? But I hope I am wrong."

She ran lightly up the steps, the others following behind. She rang the bell, but the house was dark. Maybe the occupants were abed. She rang again and then knocked loudly, but there was still no noise or sign of movement even after a few minutes.

"It is odd that a servant or butler wouldn't be up at this time," Freddie whispered in the dark.

"Then we shall have to see for ourselves." Ember tried the door, but it was locked, so she drew out her lockpicks and set to work.

"Keep watch," she uttered as she knelt in front of the door. Tilda and Sam looked out onto the street while Freddie just stared at her.

"Still invisible?" she whispered to him.

"I, er, um ..." he mumbled but looked away. Ember huffed a smile to herself. He was becoming slightly more bearable, just slightly.

After a couple of minutes, the lock clicked open. "Ah, got it," she said mostly to herself and opened the door. Holding it for the others to slip inside, she quietly closed it again.

They stood in a large hallway with a chequered black and white tiled floor. "No noise," she said in the darkness as they all stood for a moment, letting their eyes get used to the gloom. The house had a stale smell like it hadn't been lived in for a while.

Ember looked around in the darkness. Something didn't seem right, the house was too silent, not so much sleeping as holding its breath. She decided they needed to explore. "Let's pair up," she whispered. "Sam and Freddie, you take the basement and the servants' quarters and Tilda and I will search this level. Meet back here in ten minutes."

They all silently nodded their ascent and the guys headed off. Ember and Tilda turned towards the first door off the hallway that appeared to be a parlour. There was a faint layer of dust over everything, but there were also some signs of recent occupation. Tilda picked up a newspaper that was laying on a small table, and showed Ember. Ember noted the date was two days ago, but wasn't sure what to make of that.

There was nothing further to discover in the room, nor the dining room that led off it, nor in a pretty back room. It appeared to be yet another parlour, but more feminine than the first, leaving Ember to assume it was where Miss Ashton spent her time. They were soon back in the hall, with just one more door leading off, the heavy wood door was closed. As Ember opened it the first thing that struck her was the smell. There was a foetid fug to the room which seemed to almost have its own substance. Her hand flew to cover the mouth as she nearly gagged, her eyes starting to water. She turned to look at Tilda who had her own hand to her mouth, but was looking past Ember and into the room, her eyes wide.

The curtains were not drawn. Light came from the gaslight outside and spilled across a form lying on the floor.

Ashton.

He was laid with one arm over his head, the other by his side, with his hand stuck in a claw shape. His legs were as if he had just fallen, with one twisted behind the other. But the most noticeable feature was his chest. It was ripped open and there was a gaping hole where his heart should have been. A line of dried blood trailed across his once white shirt and pooled on the floor underneath him.

Ember felt despair hollow out her insides and a tightness settled across her own chest. She really had failed them all. She had gotten it completely wrong with Miss Ashton. How had she missed that it was Ashton himself who might be the target? She still thought Miss Ashton was in danger and she hadn't been able to stop the baron. He had escaped. Her first attempt at being a hunter had been disastrous. She was a disgrace to her mother's legacy. She blew out a breath, trying to stop the tears that were beginning to form.

She heard a gasp behind her and whipped round, but it was only Sam and Freddie who, having finished searching downstairs, had come to find them.

"Is that ...?" asked Freddie, looking like he was about to vomit. Ember took a breath and squared her shoulders. She might have failed, but she still had to deal with this. She nodded at Freddie.

"Gods," he whispered and turned away. Ember looked at Sam, "Did you find anything?"

He shook his head, "There is no one here, but it looks like there was until recently. There is still food in the house and some of it hasn't even been cleared away. It almost seems like the servants left in a hurry."

"We found a two day old newspaper," said Tilda, "so we can assume he was still alive then."

"Sam and I saw him only two days ago. To think that this would happen ..." Ember still couldn't believe it. "We should search the rest of the house," Ember said. "Check there is no one else here, alive or dead." She stood and looked down at Ashton, "He is not going anywhere for a while."

A short while later they had completed the search of the house and found nothing and no one else. They had joined together back in the study, still appalled by what they saw but also unwilling to leave the body alone, as if they could provide some comfort by simply being there.

"What now?" asked Freddie.

Ember didn't know what to do next. She had never seen a dead human body before. She looked at Ashton's still form, still reeling from the fact she saw him alive and well only a few days ago. "We ought to report this to the police, but I am not sure who we should tell. Sam, we aren't far from home. Can you fetch Daniel? If anyone knows, he does." Sam nodded and promised to be back as soon as possible.

As they waited for Sam to return, they had a look round the study to see if there was anything that might tell them where Miss Ashton and the baron were heading, but found nothing of importance.

Sam had taken the carriage and was not gone long before bringing Daniel back. Her mentor rushed into the room gasping, "Sam said there had been an incident." He strode over to Ember as quickly as his limp would allow and took her hands. "Are you all right?"

She nodded, gently squeezing his hands in gratitude. "Yes, thank you for coming. I didn't know what to do." He glanced at Tilda and Freddie, who were standing together across the other side of the room, then looked grimly at the body. "This is a sad thing. Sam mentioned you said his sister knew?"

"Yes, and she didn't seem very upset. Who do we report it to?" Ember asked.

"We do have to report it," Daniel sighed. He went out to the carriage and gave a name and address to the driver. "There is just one person who I trust with this," he explained as he returned. "Now tell me about what happened tonight."

Ember recounted all of the night's adventures with some interjections from the rest of the team.

"I am glad you are all okay," said Daniel, looking around them all.

"But we failed, I failed," Ember said, jaw clenched, unable to meet anyone's eyes.

❖

"I have never seen anything like this and I have seen a few sights I can tell you." The young man stood up from examining the body. He had been introduced to Ember as Inspector Arthur Stephenson. He looked to be in his mid twenties, tall and well built. He sported a neat uniform and smartly cut brown hair. The others had been ushered into the parlour as it was starting to get crowded in the study.

"And you found the body?" Arthur asked, regarding Ember with steady dark brown eyes.

"Yes, with my friend Til—Lady Margaret Fordingworth."

"Can I ask what you were doing here?"

"Well, we were looking for Ashton."

"You two young ladies were looking for a dead man in the middle of the night?" the man asked incredulously.

Ember looked at Daniel, but he just stood, both hands leaning on his cane in front of him, wearing an amused expression.

"Freddie and Sam were with us."

"And they are?" Arthur pressed, his patience visibly waning.

"Freddie is Lord Frederick Fordingworth, Lady Margaret's brother, and Sam is Samuel Hinton, my friend and neighbour."

"Let me get this straight—four young people in ..." He gestured towards Ember's fine dress, which was now looking a little rumpled and dirty from the night's activities. "All their finery, came here to look for a dead man?"

"We didn't know he was dead, but we thought he might be."

"Did you? What gave you that idea?"

"It was something his sister had said," Ember explained, starting to realise just how inconceivable it all sounded.

"Did you know the gentleman?"

"No, I did not."

"I see." The man's voice was severe as he narrowed his eyes at her.."And was the house open when you arrived? Who let you in?"

"It was locked."

"So you broke in?"

"I didn't break anything." Ember sounded offended.

"Did it ever occur to you, Miss Merrington," Arthur said sternly, "that in your rush here with all your friends to follow up a hunch based on the comments of another person, that this might be a job for the police?"

Ember flushed red, her face feeling hot and her palms sticky. She had not.

"I—no sir, I did not."

Ember looked at Daniel, appealing for his help, but he resolutely refused to look at her. She knew she had acted without thinking and that he wasn't going to help her out. This was a lesson she needed to learn on her own.

"Do you realise the evidence you have destroyed tramping all over this crime scene?"

"I am sorry sir," Ember said, "but I know who did this." She gestured towards Ashton's body.

This time it was Arthur who looked towards Daniel.

"She is a hunter, she has the gift," he offered by way of explanation.

"Ah," Arthur nodded in understanding. "Still, running

around like a group of reckless vigilantes is not how it is done. Are you training her?"

Daniel ran a hand over his face, "Trying to."

Arthur sighed and softened a little, "Once I have gotten this body moved, you had better tell me everything and I want to question your friends. I will have a report to write."

Ember exhaled the breath she had been holding, grateful she wasn't in more trouble. But he had been right and his words stung—she had behaved recklessly.

Chapter Twenty-Seven

Ember paced the kitchen, her father sat in a chair near the fire, Tilda and Freddie had arrived and had taken the other chairs, Sam sat on the floor, and Daniel leant against the doorway.

They had all arrived home in the early hours of the morning. Ember had sent the twins home, told Sam to get some sleep, and arranged for them to all meet back at lunchtime.

Ember herself had hardly slept. She had been exhausted and fallen into bed, but had awoken a short time later, haunted by the spectre of failure. Nothing the baron did—either now or in the past—hinted that Ashton was in danger, yet she couldn't shake the feeling that his death was her fault. But it was with some pride that she looked around the room. They were her friends and they were a team.

"How do we go after the baron?" she asked. "Miss Ashton is still in danger."

"We don't," replied Daniel levelly. "He will be in France by now. How can you track him there? And Miss Ashton knew what had happened to her own brother."

Ember shot him an icy look, "She was under the influence of the baron. There is still hope."

"You are such a good person, Ember," Robert added. "But not everyone can be saved."

"I refuse to give up." Ember started pacing again. "If I could have just worked it out sooner."

"What is done is done," said Daniel. "You did your best."

"Well, it wasn't good enough," said Ember fiercely, ignoring the grim look passing between Daniel and her father. She didn't mention the baron's words, that he could be back for her at some point.

"So what can we do?" asked Freddie.

Ember stopped and regarded them all, "We keep fighting. You all heard Inspector Stephenson last night—there are more and more odd cases happening in this city. Its people need protection."

Inspector Stephenson, after his grilling of Ember, had been very efficient the previous night, or rather earlier that morning. He had arranged for the body to be moved, and had said he would write up the report, but with more cases of the unexplained happening, there were very few officers he could trust with this sort of information. It was making his job harder.

"How can we fight?" Sam asked sadly. "We don't have anywhere to train, we have no money, no support."

"That is where I may be able to help." They all turned towards the source of the voice.

Lady Peyton stood in the doorway. Freddie shot out of his chair and offered it to the old lady, who smiled and accepted it gracefully. Sitting proudly, she looked round them all.

"I have been thinking I need to invest my money in something useful, and I would like to support a worthy cause. I intend to become your patron. I will provide money for you to carry on. We will charge those who can afford it and help those who cannot. I have been impressed with what you have done so far." She tilted her head towards Daniel. "Mr Beresford has kept me informed of your progress."

Ember gave Daniel a look of gratitude. He smiled and inclined his head slightly.

Ember turned back to Lady Peyton, "Thank you, but we didn't win—"

Lady Peyton held up her hand, "A minor setback, you will prevail, with the proper guidance and training." Ember felt a warmth spread throughout her body as Lady Peyton smiled at her. The woman's faith in her restored some of her own self-belief.

"I would also like to extend my house to you for training, there is plenty of room in the grounds and outbuildings. And you young man," she turned her gaze to Sam, "I have heard that you are a talented inventor."

Sam looked shocked and shot a glance at Daniel who coloured slightly and would not meet his eyes.

"I ... I think my talents have been exaggerated, ma'am," he stammered.

"Nonsense, you just need the right backing. I have a large workshop you can use."

Sam looked overjoyed and thanked her profusely.

Lady Peyton looked pleased. "That's settled then. I am looking forward to being the first director of the Bureau of the Unexplained."

"I think that name needs some work," said Ember, scrunching her nose.

Lady Peyton gave her a sharp look, "I think I can call it what I like." But there was a smile behind her words.

"Lady Peyton ..." began Ember.

"I would like you to still call me Aunt Louisa, and that goes for all you young people," she said, setting them all with a gaze.

"Aunt Louisa, thank you, this is too much, I—" Ember took a deep breath in an attempt to quiet the emotions that were threatening to spill over. "I don't know how I can repay you." She felt she would never be able to repay her. She wondered if Lady Peyton even knew what this meant—what she had really offered her.

With a knowing smile, Lady Peyton replied, "I think you will do just fine."

Acknowledgments

There are many people, without whom this book would not have been possible.

Thank you to Sarah B for listening to me wittering on and for thinking all my ideas are Netflix worthy. Special thanks to Tayler for not only being a fabulous editor, but for believing in this story from the start, for supporting me and being the best cheerleader a writer can have, I am also privileged to call her friend. And last but definitely not least thank you to my husband for putting up with and supporting my crazy.

Stay in touch
https://www.instagram.com/wlarkingbooks
https://www.facebook.com/wlarkingbooks
https://wendylarking.com

About the Author

Wendy Larking is a British author who lives on the East Coast. She has been writing since she was old enough to hold a pen and has written several short stories as well as non-fiction articles for magazines and journals.

She specialises in historical fantasy books. The Book of Secrets and Shadows is her first novel.